Other books by Chuck Dixon

LEVON CADE
Levon's Trade
Levon's Night
Levon's Ride
Levon's Run
Levon's Kin

BAD TIMES
Cannibal Gold
Blood Red Tide
Avenging Angels
Helldorado
Sons of Heaven

Gomers
Shrinkage

SIDEWINDERS
Snakehand

Seal Team Six: The Novel
Seal Team Six 2
Seal Team Six 3
Seal Team Six 4

Winterworld: The Mechanics Song
Batgirl/Robin Year One
Batman Versus Bane

• 1 •

This wasn't the first time I woke up in a cheap motel wondering how I got there. After three rough divorces I know the turf. Only not a shack-up as cheap as the one I found myself in this time.

I opened my eyelids as far as I was able. Stained ceiling tiles. Never a good sign. Drop ceilings hide things like mold or bullet holes. I tried to raise my head for a better view. Bad move. Nausea. The room shimmied like I was seeing it in a home video. Caught a glimpse of the plastic alarm clock on the nightstand before my head dropped back on the pillow.

1:21.

AM or PM?

That's how hungover I was.

Only this was like no hangover I've ever had. I've had the dry heaves hangovers. And the ones where your tongue feels like it's been replaced with a dead slug. And the ones where your eyes can't seem to look in the same direction. And the headaches. The epic, put-me-out-of-my-misery skullbangers that feel like they're never going to go away.

This one was nothing like any of them.

I felt like my body had no weight to it. Something like a tingling chill over my whole body but not unpleasant. My head felt funny but there was no pain. No headache at all. I tried to remember what I'd been drinking. The taste in my mouth was tinny. Whatever I'd been abusing the night before, it wasn't my usual.

It took a year and a half but I managed to turn on my side to face the front of the motel room. A sliver of yellow light under the drawn blinds. Afternoon then.

The room was grim. And it reeked. My nose took in every funky smell like they were in high definition. Spilled beer, cigarettes, sweat and sex. And something else. A dense, organic smell that was sweet and musky all at the same time.

Walls covered in cheap paneling that shared the secrets concealed by the ceiling tiles. An old Samsung TV was secured to the wall with a bicycle lock. An ancient chest of drawers dotted with cigarette burns. Yard sale paintings of horses crooked on the walls.

And blood.

There were dried drops on my pillow. I lifted the once-white sheet to find a broad smear of blood fringed with red fingerprints. Some of it was still tacky. The bed was sticky under me. My naked ass came off the sheets with a ripping sound.

Something barreled up my throat from my stomach. I made it to the bathroom, sliding on my knees over the cracked tiles. I tore the shower curtain aside to empty my guts into the tub.

More blood.

I vomited up what looked like a gallon of blood. Bright red with black clots sliding down the walls of the tub toward the drain.

I was dying. Right?

I ran a shaking hand over my sides and back. No stiches there. No one had taken any vital organs from me. My fingers found a wound on the side of my throat. Two crossed slits about two inches long with the flesh at the edges puckered. Someone had cut my throat and left me for dead.

My hand came back without blood on it. Maybe I was all out of blood. Maybe I was bleeding out internally. I had no idea then how much blood an adult male holds. I do now. But then I figured I must have puked up most of my supply.

On shaking legs I levered myself off of the side of the tub to get a better look at that cut on my neck.

I didn't get that far.

Scrawled across the glass of the mirror were words spelled out in blood. My blood.

WELCOME TO THE CLUB

• 2 •

I was thirty-two on the day I died.

No need for names. Not like I'm ever going to be able to use my name again.

I worked as a real estate agent at Handley and Barker. Some new home sales in the developments off the interstate. Places with names like The Oaks and The Homes at Westham. And some existing houses closer to the city.

I do okay.

Did okay. That's all over now.

I showered the blood out of the tub and ran hot water for myself. Even a blistering shower didn't take the edge off the chill I was feeling. The room filled with steam. The bloody letters ran down the face of the mirror. I toweled off and went back into the room.

My clothes were thrown all over the carpet. Business casual and my bright blue blazer with the H&B logo on the breast pocket. Most surprising to me that my wallet and keys were still in the pockets of my slacks. The cards and cash right where I left them.

I sat naked on the edge of the bed, waiting for a pot of coffee to finish brewing in the cheapjack coffee maker. Even crap "complimentary" motel coffee loaded with sugar would go a long way toward fixing me up.

I tried to put together the string of events that brought me to the Mountville Motor Lodge. The name was stamped on all the towels.

The last thing I recalled with any clarity was leaving the Essex, a bar in the first floor of the Marriot on Route One. I'd made a sale the day before and won a bet. Larry and Peter bet me I'd never sell that rundown shitshack in Overton. I made the sale to a stupid pair of newlyweds and closed the day before. Larry and Peter owed me drinks and dinner over that. Mostly drinks. Though we did stay long enough to close the Ruth's Chris before heading for the Essex.

We closed the Essex, too, and parted company in the parking lot. Larry and Peter shared a cab. I swore to get a ride. But there was no way in hell I was paying cab fare to my condo way out in Bexley. It took me three tries to get the right number and I summoned an Uber driver on my phone. Twenty minutes later a beat-to-crap Kia pulled up to the curb of the Marriot.

The driver was not the college-aged guy I usually got on Uber. And she looked out of place in the banger she was driving. She looked like she'd be way more at home on a Harley. Hair dyed indigo black and cropped blunt at the neck. Her exposed ears gleamed with rows of piercings. She wore a black t-shirt ripped to reveal her midriff. Black jeans and boots both trimmed with silver flourishes. The dark clothes set off her milk-white skin. She revealed a generous amount of cleavage when she leaned across the front seat to push the door open for me. On one breast was a small tattoo of what looked like a hieroglyph, a stylized human eye.

"Bexley?" she said. She had a trace of a French accent. That sealed the deal for me. I was in lust.

"Yeah."

I folded myself into the seat next to her. She floored it off the Marriot lot, my door slamming shut.

"You're cute," she said. The Kia puttered down Commercial Avenue.

"I'm drunk," I said.

"Just drunk or drunk enough?" She smiled as she drove, eyes on me.

I was trying to get my head around her question when she spoke again.

"You in a hurry to get home?"

It was all a hash after that. I could recall glimpses of a parade of bars and clubs. The order was fuzzy but I sensed that we moved down the chain of drinking places to the bottom. I recall Roxanne—that was the Uber driver's name—getting into it with a pair of bikers at a place called Loki's. No idea how that turned out. Lost somewhere in my alcohol delirium.

The room I found myself in was featured in a few scattered moments I could dredge up. I remember rolling on the bed naked with Roxanne, our clothes thrown everywhere in the frenzy to get at each other. The one thing that was clear in my memory was the girl holding me down on the bed and me fighting to get at the teacup breasts swinging free just before my nose. She was strong, far stronger than her skinny body led me to expect. The last thing I remember was her on top of me, lips close to my ear, a throaty chuckle as she whispered.

"Want to try something *really* wild?"

Wild, all right. Waking up alone with my throat slit, puking blood and a threatening message painted on the bathroom mirror. The worst of it was, I thought, that I couldn't remember any of the sex.

What did it mean? *Welcome to the club.* Did she have some wicked STD that she shared with me? Herpes. Jesus, maybe AIDS. The bitch left me with something that might kill me, I was sure of it.

I would need treatment. I considered calling 911. Then thought more about it. Did I want a police report on file to document this whole thing? I wasn't robbed. The wound on my throat wasn't fatal. That blood I puked up could be from an ulcer. I'd look like a grade-A asshole. I'd get a cab to take me back to the Marriot to get my car. I had a showing at three. A four-bed-two-bath in Hunter's Court. I could make it. A little rumpled and shaky, but I could make it.

I might be able to make it by without a shave. I went into the bathroom to take a look.

I was struck again by the message on the glass, now running streaked down the surface on rivulets of condensation.

I was struck more by what I saw in the mirror behind the words. Nothing. I mean, I saw an empty motel bathroom and nothing else.

No me.

It was like I wasn't there.

I was touching my fingers to the wet glass when the banging on the door began.

• 3 •

It was a guy from the motel office. That's how he announced himself between hammering on the door with his fist.

"Motel office!"

I wrapped a towel around my waist and went to open the door a crack.

A blinding light came through the gap making me stumble back against the bed. And I *mean* blinding. I couldn't see a thing except exploding sparks of white brilliance. I threw an arm across my face. A stinging sensation washed over every inch of exposed skin. The persistent chill was gone, replaced with a scorching heat as if I'd touched a hot iron.

"You only paid one night. It's way after check-out."

"Damn." I rubbed at my eyes with my fists. The white sparklers were replaced by red dots against black.

"Stay after eleven it's another day," the guy said, stepping into the room.

"Could you close the door behind you?" I waved a free hand at him. My arm was still across my eyes to shut out the painful glare coming off the parking lot.

"Bad night, huh?" He said it without amusement.

"Weird night," I said. I lay back on the bed, feeling the burning sensation leave my face and chest.

"If you're staying you're paying."

"My wallet. In my pants." I waved the hand toward the chair where my slacks hung folded. I heard him cross the room to the chair.

"Take what you need."

"It's seventy-five. All's you got is twenties."

"Have mercy, man. Take eighty and get out of here."

I heard the bills crumple. I turned away as he crossed to the door. Even with my back to the door and both hands pressed over my eyes I could see the new burst of sunlight. And that scorching sensation climbed up my spine, growing in intensity, until I heard the door click shut.

I lay back on the bed, face to the ceiling, eyes pressed shut.

The coffee maker dinged. My mini-pot of motel coffee was brewed.

I got up, legs shaking, and poured a cup then dumped in three sugars. Halfway to my nose the smell of coffee filled my nose and mouth. Usually one of the most welcome moments of the day, right? Not today. Instead of the nutty aroma of fresh brewed, a cloying mustiness crawled down my throat making my stomach heave. I threw the cup aside to spatter over the paneling.

Falling back on the bed, I curled up into a ball. A deep agony clawed at my guts brought on by the smell of the coffee. My knees to my chest and shivering, I began to cry like a baby. I was wracked with a sobbing that made the box springs squeal under me. Only my eyes were dry. No tears came.

No blood. No tears.

What the hell had that bitch given me?

Decided to try an experiment.

I stripped the bed to cover my head and body with the sheets and the spread. I probably looked like some kind of half-assed costume Arab. No way to tell since I couldn't see myself in a mirror.

Blinded by the bedclothes covering my head, I stumbled to the door of the room. I fumbled with the door knob and pushed the door open as far as the chain lock would allow. I bared one hand and arm and stuck it out into the afternoon sun.

I stood the searing pain as long as I could before pulling it back in and slamming the door tight again.

My hand and arm, from the fingertips to above my elbow, was black with gray flecks of ash lying atop it. The first layer of skin was singed and already peeling away to leave dead white flesh beneath. And it hurt like hell. I ran cold water over it with no relief. The only thing that helped was sitting in the dark until the pain faded away. The hand and arm remained black though.

I saw something on TV once about a kid who couldn't go outside because the sunshine would kill him. But that was an allergy or some other kind of condition that the kid was born with. It wasn't something you could catch off some Uber driving whore.

No matter what it was, there was no way I was making my three o'clock. I rang up Handley and Barker. Glenna answered and I told her that I came down with some kind of stomach bug and could Larry or Peter take my showing? She told me she'd take care of it and suggested dry toast and weak tea before hanging up.

I collapsed back on the bed and ran everything over and over in my mind until I dropped off to sleep. Only I don't remember falling to sleep. More like passing out. Or surrendering to a trance.

• 4 •

It was full dark outside when I woke up and called a cab. No more Uber for me, thank you.

A horn honked out on the lot. I opened the door a crack to stick an experimental hand outside. No burning sensation. I stumbled out between two parked cars and dropped in through the sliding door of the bright yellow minivan.

I told the driver to take me to the Marriot where I left my car. The deep sleep I'd been in most of the day didn't leave me with a rested feeling. I had a hollow sensation inside that was different than hunger—even though I couldn't remember the last meal I ate. My head felt like a balloon on the end of string. And my vision was funny. Not blurred exactly. More like looking through heavily tinted lenses. Every light source was surrounded by a shimmering halo.

Maybe these were the first symptoms of whatever Roxanne had shared with me. Or I could have been drugged. Was this what that date rape drug was like?

"You need to buckle yourself," the driver said.

I pulled myself upright and snapped the straps in place.

I watched the back of the driver's head as he pulled off the motel lot. He had protruding ears that were translucent whenever the headlights of approaching traffic struck them. I could see even the tiniest blood vessels inside the papery lobes. I could see the veins in his neck. I could see his pulse. Swear to God I could *hear* his pulse.

The emptiness in my gut turned to fire. A sudden swirling blaze spreading out to my arms and legs. My joints felt like they had blades in them. The scalded skin on my arm broke out in a maddening itch.

"You don't look so good," the driver said.

"I'll be fine," I said. My eyes were staring, fascinated, by the throbbing artery in his neck as he turned to glance back at me.

"Just don't puke back there."

"Sure. Sure."

"If you're going to puke let me know and I'll pull over."

"Sure. Sure will."

The Impala was right where I left it the night before. The cab driver asked if I was okay to drive.

"I'm sober. Just not feeling well. Some kind of bug."

His wide eyes and slack mouth told me that I looked every bit as bad as I felt.

I got the door open first try and slid in behind the wheel. The cab pulled away. I rested my forehead on the steering wheel before gunning the motor to life.

The drive back to Bexley took an eternity. The streetlights and headlights stabbed me in the eyes. Every other surface emitted a curious glow as if the world was made of neon. I tried to blink it away. I drove to the condo through a nimbus of shifting glare.

Rather than head to my own place I knocked at the neighbors' door two down from me. Cheryl and her roommate Nancy. They were both nurses at Memorial.

Cheryl, the redhead, answered the door. She wore an over-big state college sweatshirt and sleep pants. I hoped I didn't wake her. I wasn't real clear on what time it was.

"Holy shit. Is that you?"

I practically fell into her foyer. She called for Nancy and they both helped me inside. A male voice on the TV in the living room. An audience laughing in response. They parked me on the stool at their kitchen bar.

"Get him a drink of water, Nance." Cheryl dashed deeper into the condo while Nancy opened a bottle of Fiji that I waved away. Nancy was in a pair of pajamas open at the throat to show the curve of her pink breasts. All I had eyes for was her delicate neck exposed under a fringe of short cropped honey-blonde hair. The muscles and cords under a fine layer of peach fuzz held me enthralled. I ran my tongue over my lips.

Cheryl came back with a blood pressure cuff and stethoscope. She put a hand to my forehead.

"You're ice cold. You *look* feverish though," she said.

"I feel like I'm dying," I said. It came out a croak. My throat was painfully dry all of a sudden.

Nancy helped her get the pressure cuff in place and pumped it up. They glanced at one another as it hissed itself empty. Cheryl bent to place the stethoscope drum on my arm. My eyes followed the vein in her neck to where it vanished under the collar of her sweatshirt. I breathed in through my nostrils, filling my nose with her rich scent of dewy sweat and shampoo. My ears filled with the sound of her heartbeat and the whoosh-whoosh of blood moving through her veins. I opened my eyes to find Nancy looking at me with narrowed eyes.

"Something wrong with this cuff," Cheryl said. She left it in place and held the scope against my chest. She sat back and exchanged a look with her roommate.

"You're dead, Jason," she said. Her head was lowered and tilted to one side to look me in the eyes.

"That's what I told you. I'm dying," I said.

"Died. Past tense. You have no blood pressure and no pulse. Not one I can find anyway," Cheryl said.

"Bullshit. You did it wrong," Nancy said.

"Excuse me?" Cheryl said.

Nancy took the scope from her and put the drum on my back.

"Take a deep breath and let it out," she said.

I did as she told me. Four times.

"Shit," Nancy said. She backed away to stand against the kitchen counter.

"I told you. No vitals," Cheryl said.

"We need to call 911. Or take him to the ER ourselves," Nancy said.

"No. No. No. No doctors. No hospital," I said. I climbed down off the stool and waved them back.

"Hold on . . ." Cheryl began. But I was already to their door and opening it. Both girls followed me. They tried to hold the door closed. I easily yanked it open with one hand and staggered down the hall to my door.

I made it to my own sofa to face plant in the cushions.

The burning in my guts was a five-alarm tire fire now. I curled up on the sofa clutching my stomach with clawed fingers. I still had the girls' scent in my nostrils, sweet and musky. A longing was taking over me, a desire greater than sexual. I wanted something that I couldn't have; couldn't even understand or name.

The stereo was on. The display face glowed electric green. A jazz station. Someone whisking a drum while someone else played a plaintive trumpet. I knew I didn't leave it on. I hate jazz.

A husky voice spoke from the dark.

"You got it bad, *mon petit.*"

I sat up to look over the back of the couch.

Roxanne lounged back in my favorite chair, her face lit by the red glow of a cigarette in her slim fingers.

"Why don't you let Mama help?"

• 5 •

I was over the back of the couch in a vault that surprised both of us.

Roxanne was out of the chair and backing down the hall that led to the bedrooms at the back of the condo.

"You—bitch! What did you do to me?" I said. I stalked toward her.

"What did I do *for* you, stupid," she said. The easy manner I recalled from the night before came back to her. A tilted smile on her face, her eyelids dropping over the blackest eyes I'd ever seen. I'd forgotten her eyes. Like ebony glass.

"What the hell does that mean?" I was stammering. I'd have been spitting but my mouth was dry as sand.

She moved backwards toward the bedrooms, eyes on me, her lush lips cooing words I couldn't hear through my rage. I made a leap for her, reaching for her wrists. We both crashed down on the foot of my bed. She drove a knee into my chest, knocking me tumbling.

I came back up off the carpet to find her spider walking up the mattress toward the head of the bed.

"I've got what you want, *mon sucre*," she said. I'd forgotten the trace of an accent. It would be sexy as hell under other circumstances. Right now I just wanted to cause her pain.

I launched for the bed. She rolled out from under me. I raised up to make a grab for her. From somewhere under a t-shirt for a band called Kreator she produced something that shone in the moonlight coming through drapes.

A razor blade. I grabbed a calf and pulled her closer, making a reach for the hand that held the blade. She drew closer only to head butt me. I fell back seeing flashes of iridescent stars dancing across the ceiling.

She was on top of me then, straddling my hips and holding me down with a hand to my chest. I had a good forty pounds on her but she pressed me down on the bed like I was a child.

"I've got what you need," she said. With a corner of the razor blade she sliced across the front of her t-shirt and tore the fabric aside to expose one of her breasts. The one with the Egyptian eye tattooed on it.

I rocked back and forth snarling but couldn't free myself from under her.

With a single deft stroke she made a slice across the mound of her breast above the nipple. Dark blood thick as gelatin seeped out of the wound. I stared at it, transfixed. My body went limp, all will to fight flushed out of me at the sight of the red-black stream dripping off the curve of her breast. She bent the arm that was restraining me to bend at the waist, bringing her closer to me. We lay belly to belly. She placed her hand on the back of my head and pulled my face to her chest.

"That's it, baby. Take what you need," she said. Her voice a whisper.

That urge came over me, something primal, drawing me up toward her. My nose filled with the sweet tang coming off the blood. With a wordless animal sound I clamped my lips over the wound and sucked the irresistible nectar.

I lay back on the bed staring at the ceiling. My body was warm in the afterglow of feeding and wrapped in a cocoon of utter contentment. That blaze in my guts was gone. In its place was pleasant radiance.

Roxanne sat propped against the head of the bed, lighting a cigarette. The wound was closed. It looked like a papercut now. Her breast was clean of every drop of blood. I'd made sure of that.

"You need to learn to hunt on your own," she said. She let twin streams of creamy smoke drift from her nostrils.

"What?" I said. I was trying the free myself from the lazy feeling washing over me.

"You can't be looking at me to be your mama. You'll be on your own from here."

I turned on an elbow to look at her. Her dark eyes regarded me without warmth through a blue haze of smoke. The strangeness of this woman in my bed, and what we'd just done together, was sinking in.

"What is this? Is this some kind of kinky shit? What are you into? What am *I* into?" I was sitting up now. Her tilted smile returned. Her eyes remained cold.

"You think this was *sex*? Maybe love, *mon petit*?" A dry chuckle in her throat as she said it.

"Then what is it?"

"I did not find something that was already in you. Some unrealized kink you were ignorant of before yesterday. I *changed* you. You are not who you were. Not *what* you were."

"It's not sex? What's that mean?"

"Is your cock hard?"

It was not. I'd just participated in what would normally be the ultimate wet dream; a strange exotic woman in my condo with whom I wound up rolling in bed with her tits exposed. But I was satisfied with sucking a pint of blood out of her, more satisfied than I'd ever known I could feel. And sex, actual intercourse or any of its variations, never occurred to me. I was still fully clothed.

"I am sorry," she said. Her mouth turned down. There was mock sympathy in her words. The eyes were still lifeless as a doll's.

"What is this? What did you do to me? Are you dying and wanted to infect someone with whatever you have?"

She laughed then, a throaty laugh that expelled a cloud of smoke.

"I died long ago. You died last night."

I rose to my knees to crawl closer to her. I touched my hand to her flesh, my palm between her breasts. There was no pulse.

"The others are going to be very unhappy with me," she said. She closed her eyes, black lashes joining. Her hand atop mine.

Others?

• 6 •

"Crosses?"

She snorted.

"Wooden stakes."

"No," she said.

"Do I get to turn into a bat?"

"Don't be silly," she said.

"What about Dracula? Is that a real thing?"

"Enough questions. Just drive," Roxanne said.

I was driving us along the interstate. She convinced me that I couldn't stay in my condo. I had to leave it behind. Leave my whole life up till now behind me. She told me not to take anything with me.

"Not even a change of clothes?"

"There will be plenty of clothes where we're going," she said. She waved at an exit sign and I pulled off the highway onto a surface road.

She pointed left and I turned to drive into the darkness under a double overpass. Traffic boomed by overhead.

"You know this isn't the best neighborhood," I said.

"Are you afraid?" That tilted smile again.

"I was thinking about you."

"Pull over here." She pointed to the deep shadows behind a row of concrete pylons.

I killed the motor and she climbed out. She tapped a ring on the glass and motioned for me to follow.

I walked behind her toward a collection of tents slung up in the shelter of the southbound overpass. The little tent city spread up onto a grassy slope where the highway split. There was a barrel fire going. Some of the tents glowed with lantern light. One pulsed with the bluish hues of a television screen.

Roxanne dropped to a crouch on a patch of gravel and pulled my sleeve to bring me down by her.

"We're staying here?" I said.

"We're hunting." Her eyes were locked on the tents. Nothing moved there.

"I'm not sure about this," I said.

"I need blood. You took a lot of mine. You need more yourself. And you need to learn how to make it out here on your own." She glanced at me once. The moon was reflected in her eyes making them glow pewter.

"You want us to kill someone?" I tried to stand up. She yanked me back down to my knees.

"Do you know what this place is?" she said. It was a hiss.

"Sure. Homeless people."

"Criminals. Pedophiles. Sick bastards who rape children."

"*All* of them?"

"Registered sex offenders. They can't live anywhere near where children might gather. Schools, playgrounds, daycares. This is the only place they can live and meet their parole requirements."

"I think I saw something on TV about this place."

"Did you ever see anything on TV about men from this place disappearing?"

"No," I said.

She smiled. And this time the smile went all the way to her eyes. It was not a nice smile.

Someone coughed then grunted by one of the tents. A man came out of a bright yellow tent, a flashlight in his hand. Chubby guy in an aloha shirt and cargo shorts. He came down the grassy slope and crossed the surface road toward a porta potty sitting at the curb.

Roxanne was up and moving. Her hand was clamped on my wrist to pull me along. We angled across the surface road toward a porta potty and arrived just as the chubby guy was pulling the door open. Roxanne gripped the door, holding it open. The chubby guy goggled at her at first. His face twisted into an ugly sneer and he entered the toilet, trying to pull the door closed behind him. Roxanne slapped his arm aside and joined him inside the potty. The door banged closed behind her.

I was left outside to listen to a complaint from the chubby guy followed by a short yelp. A gurgling sound came through the vents then silence. I looked to the tent village. Nothing moved. The only sound was tinny music from the television.

The door banged open and Roxanne hissed for me to come in.

She had chubby pinned to the back wall of the closet-sized room. A bloody razor blade between her fingers. She'd made a slash across the guy's neck and blood spurted from it in time with his slowing pulse. The guy's eyes were moving and his jaw was working. No sound came out and the eyes were unfocused. His legs quivered feebly.

"Come on. Don't waste any," Roxanne said. Her mouth glistened crimson. She grabbed the lapel of my blazer and tugged me closer.

I tried to brace my feet but they slid on the slick metal surface of the potty floor. She took me by the back of the head and shoved me against the dying man. My nose and mouth filled with the rich scent of the blood running down to stain the guy's hideous shirt. That fire was stoked up in my belly. I fell into a world of delirium where the only thing that existed was the stream of sweet red wine spilling from the narrow wound.

And hunger.

A hunger such as I'd never felt before.

I was feeding on the guy before I knew it.

"That's it, *mon petit*. Take it all. The dregs are always the most delicious," Roxanne said. Her fingers were still in my hair.

• 7 •

With Roxanne's directions I drove us onto the empty lot of a suburban mall. I pulled up behind a Macy's and parked. Roxanne was out of the car and climbing steel steps up to a loading dock. I chased after. She walked down the row of sealed garage doors to a steel entry door.

"What's here?" I said.

"Shopping," she said. She touched a buzzer by the door.

"You know someone inside?"

She squinted at me, annoyed.

The loading dock was quiet. The only sound was the ticking from the Impala's engine block as it cooled. The parking lot was a barren asphalt landscape dotted with pools of artificial light.

I looked down at my shirt front. It was black with blood. My blazer too, smeared where I'd wiped my sticky hands.

Roxanne touched the buzzer again. Through the door I could hear the harsh ringing of a bell.

"Won't they see us?" I said. I glanced up at a surveillance camera mounted over the door. It was trained down on us.

Roxanne shrugged.

Footsteps approached the door from inside. A jingle of key rings. The locks turned and the door came open. A balding black guy poked his head out. He wore a dark blue uniform shirt dotted with cookie crumbs.

He was surprised to see Roxanne smiling at him. Even more surprised when she latched onto his throat and shoved him inside.

The guard's feet left the floor and he slid along the tiles in a narrow hallway lined with doors. Roxanne stepped inside and stormed toward him. The guard went for a gun in a holster on his belt. He only made it as far as unsnapping the catch. Roxanne drove the heel of a boot into his face. Once. Twice. The guard lay still.

She grabbed a fistful of his collar and dragged him deeper into the building. I trotted behind.

"What are we doing with him?" I said.

"We?"

"You're going to cut his throat?"

"No. Too messy."

We reached the security office. A desk and a bank of monitors shifting between views of various interior and exterior shots all around the mall. A cooling mug of coffee and an open bag of Mrs. Fieldings sat by an open copy of a car magazine. Roxanne plopped the guard into a chair. She plucked tie-wraps from his belt and secured his wrists behind the post of the back rest. Another pair of wraps around his ankles held them unmoving against the chair legs. She undid his gun belt and threw it across the room. She tore off her own t-shirt and balled part of it up to stick in his mouth. He sagged in the chair, breath whistling from his nostrils.

"The place is ours," she said. She stepped to a panel on the wall and pressed a series of buttons. Each was marked with the name of a store.

The gates of the stores were all wide open.

We hit Macy's, Wilson Leather, and Abercrombie & Fitch. Roxanne picked out a tank top, jeans and motorcycle jacket. All in black, of course. She stripped naked at the racks to put them on. I bagged up some t-shirts, jeans, a hoodie and underwear. She slapped the bags from my hands.

"Only take what you can wear," she said.

I stripped down and put on fresh clothes, leaving my bloody shirt, slacks and Handley-Barker blazer on the floor. I walked barefoot down to the Foot Locker and snagged socks and a pair of K-Swiss high tops. I rejoined Roxanne seated on the edge of the fountain in the mall's center court.

"How do I look?" I said.

"Like an asshole." But she smiled when she said it.

"What now? I guess the food court's out."

"We need to roost," she said. She glanced up at the wide atrium dome above us. The sky was lightening to a pale violet streaked with dark clouds.

"Where do we go?"

"We're already here," she said. She took my hand.

We climbed up to a utility room on the roof and lay down on the top of a broad exchange vent. There was just enough clearance between the top of the vent and the ceiling to lay supine. The room had no windows. Roxanne had a pair of thick comforters taken from Macy's linen department. We spread them out and lay side by side.

Roxanne lit a cigarette and took a long drag. She blew out a stream that billowed against the steel plates of the ceiling inches above us.

"Is this smart? Staying here?" I said.

"No one will think to look for us here," she said.

"We just stay here all day?"

"And join the shoppers when the sun goes down."

"That camera. It couldn't see us. Like the empty mirror image."

"That's right, *mon petit*. We are invisible. None of the cameras saw us."

"I almost feel sorry for the cops who have to investigate this," I said.

She made a huffing sound that expelled a fresh plume of blue smoke. The police. What were the police to her?

We lay quiet a few moments.

"They'll find my car," I said.

"And so?"

"Right. I'm dead."

I listened to the whump of a transformer kicking on and the whoosh of air moving through the vent below us for a few moments. I felt warm all over, a heat spreading from my belly. It sloshed with the blood of the pedophile.

"What is that you call me? Mon puh-teet? That's like calling me a child, isn't it?"

"To me you are a child, *sucre*."

"Come on. You're younger than me? What? Twenty-two? For sure you're not thirty yet."

That dry chuckle again. I turned to see her smiling in the red glow of the cigarette clamped between her lips. Her eyes were on the ceiling.

"How old *are* you, Roxanne?" I said. My voice was small in the dark.

"I saw the walls come down."

"You mean in Berlin? That was almost thirty years ago."

"In Paris," she said. A ghost of a whisper.

I searched my mind for anything like what she was talking about. Like a light switch being flipped, my thoughts evaporated into tranquil blackness.

• 8 •

We came down from the utility room and joined the evening crowd wandering the mall. Roxanne took a seat at the Este Lauder counter in Macy's. A pretty blonde cosmetics rep came around the counter to help her.

I walked away to wander the mall a while. Just before closing we joined up again. Roxanne was laughing. She had fresh blush on her cheeks. Her eyes were made up with blue shadow and her lips were coated in deep red smeared slightly at the corners.

"Something funny?" I said.

"The girl said she wished she had skin like mine," she said.

"And what did you say?"

"Nothing. I just did this." She grabbed me by the back of the head and jammed her lips to mine, her tongue prying my teeth apart to explore my palate. She released me to stumble back and bent double in mirth.

My car was where we left it behind the mall. An orange sticker on the window. An impound order. But the county tow truck hadn't shown up and I still had my key ring.

We climbed into the Impala and drove away.

The fire was building in my guts again. I needed to feed. I looked over at Roxanne in the flickering glare of the streetlights. There were lines around her mouth that weren't there before. She was feeling the hunger, too.

"We'll go back to the tent city," she said.

"No. I'm not feeding off some pervert in a rent-a-shitter," I said. I powered up the ramp onto the turnpike.

"Blood is blood."

"Leaving bodies all over town is not a good idea."

"They are suicides. Sad men who cut their throats rather than live with the shame of their desires."

Their desires? Funny.

"The police are going to start noticing if lots of sex offenders start turning up dead," I said.

"Then we move to another place. The world is ours. The night belongs to us," she said.

That had the feel of something she'd said before.

"I have a better idea," I said. I veered over two lanes and down the ramp for Arlington.

"You're going to steal from a blood bank," Roxanne said.

"That's right," I said.

We were parked in the visitor lot outside North Hillside Hospital.

"Do you think you are the first to think of this?" she said.

"I just don't feel like killing someone tonight."

She made a scoffing noise.

"Unless they turn like I did. Did the pervert last night join the club, too?"

"No," she said. She lit a cigarette, face white in the glare of the lighter.

"What was different?"

"I let you drink my blood. That makes you like me. Like us."

"Why? Why me?"

"I don't know. Perhaps I saw something in you, *mon petit*. Maybe it was something you said. Maybe because you didn't bore me. Not like you are boring me now." A stream of smoke struck the windshield.

"I'll be right back," I said. I climbed out of the Impala and left her smoking. I wondered if she'd be there when I returned.

In the hospital lobby a woman with blue hair reminded me that visiting hours were over. She didn't look up from the solitaire game on her phone. I found the elevators and entered a car. I pressed for the fourth floor and exited to find one sign pointing to maternity and another toward oncology and radiology.

"Can I help you?" It was a nurse pushing a med cart toward the elevators. She didn't sound like she was in a helpful mood. Her question had more of the tone of "Where the hell do you think you're going?"

"I got a call. About my mother," I said.

"What is she here for?" The nurse brought the cart to a stop.

"Cancer. Stage four. They told me I should come in."

Her face softened. She was pretty now. I saw her eyes glisten wetly. Then I watched the artery in her throat throbbing with the rhythm of life. Her voice brought me out of my momentary fixation.

"You want ICU. That's down on two," she said.

"Thank you," I said. I pressed the down button.

"I'll say a prayer for your mother," she said. She pushed on with the med cart.

"That's very kind," I said and stepped through the opening doors.

Intensive care. That was a sure place to find blood, right? All kinds.

Trouble was it was locked down tight. The only way in was through a pair of automatic doors operated from inside by the nurses at the duty desk. I stepped back from the doors to walk a hallway that ended in a kind of lounge with tables and chairs and the Food Channel playing mutely on a wall-mounted TV. Against one wall was a row of vending machines. I bought four coffees and walked back to ICU where I stood looking through the panes of the locked doors, wearing a pleading look. The four paper cups of scalding liquid held in an awkward grip. An Asian nurse in pink scrubs spotted me and took mercy. The doors cranked open. I scooted past the duty desk with a grateful smile. The nurse nodded back, pleased to be of help. I hurried on deeper into the unit toward some imaginary destination; some aggrieved family in desperate need of caffeine and sugar.

Once out of sight around the corner I dropped the coffees into a medical waste bin.

The ICU was dimmer than the rest of the hospital. The only source of illumination was the indirect lighting coming from panels along the ceiling and the readouts on the machines. The machines beeped and booped alongside the beds of patients inside rooms separated from the hallway by glass-lined walls.

Past the rooms was a second hallway that branched to the right to end twenty or thirty feet along. There were doorways either side. A unisex bathroom for visitors. A break room with a table and chairs, a mini-fridge and a coffeemaker. A linen closet. Last room along had no marking on it. The fluorescents in the ceiling kicked on when I opened the door.

There was an empty med cart and some kind of equipment on wheels covered with a cloth. Cabinets lined the walls and an open shelf was stacked with bins loaded with boxes of gauze, syringes and other bits of medical necessities in cellophane packets. At the back of the room was a white refrigerator. I pulled it open to find it stacked with boxes of tiny glass vials and, hanging from steel racks, were rows of plastic blood packs.

I felt a pinch in my stomach. My tongue moved across my teeth. I felt that heat rising behind my eyes. My nose filled with the scent of blood even through the sealed packets.

I searched the room for anything I could use as a carry-all. I wound up dumping out a box of vials into a trash bin. They fell in with a tinkling sound. I dropped to my knees to scoop blood packs into the box as fast as I could manage.

"What the fuck?" A deep voice growling with rising anger behind me.

An enormous man in purple scrubs was braced in the room's only door. The knuckles on his meaty hands were turning white where they gripped the door and jamb.

• 9 •

The guy came at me like a bear. Or a wrestler. Or a wrestling bear.

All I could think of was slipping past him without him getting a hold of me. Impossible in the narrow room with his three hundred pound bulk between me and the door.

He halved the distance between us. I moved with a speed I didn't know I was capable of. He was LeBron and I was a runaway jump ball. I moved from wall to wall, ducking under his arms. He caught me in one mile-wide hand and slammed me against a wall of cabinets. The guy was holding me up with a hand over my face and another locked on my arm. My sneakers were squeaking on the tiles until he lifted me clear of the floor.

My last fight was in the sixth grade. I got my ass kicked. By a girl.

I opened my mouth and bit down hard into the meat at the web of his hand. A spray of blood shot up into my face. It tasted like cooked onions and another aftertaste. Cilantro. The guy howled and leapt back. I dropped to the floor and landed a punch that split his nose in two. A fresh gout of hot blood. He collapsed against the wall unconscious.

I scooped up the box of blood packs, hopped over the sleeping giant and was out the door and out of the ICU in what felt like three steps. The nurse in pink had no time to look up before I was gone from sight and down the stairwell for the ground.

"You had trouble," Roxanne said.

I threw the box of blood packs into the Impala and jumped behind the wheel. The sound of sirens was getting louder as I swerved us off the lot. Roxanne took one of my hands. She licked the orderly's blood from my knuckles. I took my foot off the gas. The Impala was moving five miles under the speed limit when a chain of cop cars, sirens screaming and lights twirling, passed us heading for the hospital.

Roxanne sorted through the box. She tossed packs out the open window.

"Do you know what I went through to get those?" I said.

"Plasma's no good. Only whole blood," she said.

She tried to open a pack and spilled a gout of blood over her face. I laughed. She waggled the pack at me, drizzling me claret red. I picked up a pack and bit the plastic nipple open and sucked down the chilled syrup. She did the same, lounging back in her seat, head tilted back to squeeze the bag's contents into her mouth. We rolled on down a golden mile lined with darkened strip malls and car dealerships. It reminded me of the time me and Ricky Gotshall drove around drinking a six-pack of Heinies he stole from his dad's garage.

"Fresh is better," she said.

"You sound like one of those assholes at Whole Foods," I said.

"This blood is shit. All mixed up. You know that, don't you? A cocktail pumped from a thousand veins. I like to feed from one source."

"It does the job."

It did do the job. The blaze in my gut was tamped down to warming embers.

She glanced at the time on my dash.

"We need to roost," she said.

"Yeah. I have a few ideas about that," I said.

"I don't want your ideas, *mon petit*. We cannot sleep just anywhere."

"I thought we were outlaws. There are rules now?"

"There are rules. We cannot enter any place we have not been to before. Or where we are not invited first."

"That's for real?"

"It is for real."

"What about the mall? The hospital? Those bars we went to after I picked you up?"

"You picked *me* up?" She smiled at that. The wind through the window tossed her feather-fine hair.

"What about those places?"

"They are public places. Anyone is welcome, silly."

"Well, I want to sleep in a real bed. Not in some crawlspace like a cockroach," I said.

"And where is this?" Her smile faded. Roxanne was no longer amused by my boyish charm.

"Did I tell you I was a realtor?"

I pulled up into the driveway and cut the engine in front of the three-car garage of 1164 McIntosh Drive in Applewood Estates. The five-bed/three-bath mini-mansion sat on one of the lanes that wound through the gated development. All the streets were named for brands of apples. There was Gala Street and Winesap Way. Probably an idea from the developer's wife.

"This won't work," Roxanne said. She stayed in her seat when I got out of the car.

"And why not? The place is unoccupied. The owners moved to Pittsburgh last month. I have the key to the lockbox," I said.

"You have not been invited to this house. You told me you've never been here," she said.

"So? It's multi-listed." I pointed at the For Sale sign down by the curb. The Taylor Group's logo and phone number were on the board.

"I don't know what that means." She was leaning from the window as I popped the trunk.

"It means that, as a rep for Handley-Barker, I have a right to show this house. I'm welcome here contractually." I snagged my laptop bag from the floor of the trunk.

"It won't work. It is not the same," she said. She worked the lever and dropped her seat back to a recline position.

I was at the double front doors and undid the lockbox hanging from the latch. The key to the house dropped into my hand. I worked in the knob lock and deadbolt and pushed the door open. The foyer lay within. Hardwood floors, crown molding. A carpeted flight of steps led to the second floor. A full gourmet kitchen lay in the darkness at the end of a corridor leading from the rear of the foyer to the back of the house.

I hesitated. Roxanne hadn't told me what would happen if I tried to enter a house uninvited. Was there an invisible force field preventing me from stepping inside? Would I catch fire? Turn to dust? Bounce back into the middle of McIntosh Drive?

"Fuck it," I said.

I stepped onto the faux Oriental area rug inside. There was still the tang of fresh baked chocolate chip cookies hanging in the air from the last open house. I walked back out to the Impala and leaned into the driver's window.

"May I show you the house, ma'am?"

She glared at me through slitted eyes.

• 10 •

"This house isn't scheduled for a showing until next week," I said.

"I still don't like it," she said.

I closed the laptop. I was cross-legged on the queen bed in the master bedroom. Naked from a shower to rinse the dried blood off me. Roxanne entered from the master bath, naked as well. Our clothes were downstairs in the washer.

The owners were gone. The house was staged by the listing agency with rented furniture. It was like we were playing house. We went through the rooms drawing blinds and shades. In the master bedroom we covered the windows with comforters and tablecloths secured in place with a roll of duct tape I found in the garage.

"I think we should sleep in the attic," she said.

She sat toweling off her legs on the edge of the bed. Her damp hair shone like onyx where it was plastered to the milk-white skin at the back of her neck.

"And miss the chance to lay in a bed?" I moved closer to her, running my hands down her spine. My fingers brushed over a puckered scar at the small of her back. She dropped back to lie supine on the bed. I leaned down to kiss her. She returned the kiss, drawing my tongue between her teeth.

Something clamped on my balls and twisted hard. I pulled away. Roxanne had my testicles in the grip of one hand. Her face was twisted in furious delight.

"Do you feel that, *mon petit*?" she said. It came out in a hiss.

"Shit," I said, gasping for air. I grabbed her wrist. She twisted harder.

She rolled closer, her face inches from mine. Her bottle-glass eyes on mine.

"That is *all* you will feel. That need is over for you. It is replaced by a different fire."

She released me and I rolled away, falling to the floor by the bed. She rose from the bed to pick up her cigarettes from the vanity. She sat in a faux Queen Anne chair with a plush cushion and lit up. The smoke from her lips was visible in the triptych of mirrors against the background of an empty room. She studied the glass as though looking for something there.

"We are neuters. I am barren. You are a gelding. The hunger is the only urge that matters. We *are* hunger. We are its creature."

"Like slaves," I said. The pain in my crotch faded to a dull ache. I dropped back on the bed.

"Who is not a slave to something? Did you like selling other people's homes? Did you love your silly jacket with other men's names on it?"

"I got paid. I got something in exchange for my work. What do I get out of this?"

She turned to me, eyes smoky under bangs slick with damp.

"You get to live forever." She turned away.

"Is that for real? We don't die? I'm just going to go on and on?"

"Until someone stops you, *mon petit*."

I lay back on the bed atop the brocaded spread.

"But I live like this. Alone except for you. Never seeing daylight. Either in a coma or hungry. I'm not sure this is such a great deal."

"It isn't."

"Then why did you make me like this?"

I felt the mattress move under me. She was beside me on the

bed, her head resting on my shoulder, a leg thrown over my stomach. Her long nails played over my chest.

"Maybe I was lonely, *mon petit*."

I didn't say anything. I was still dealing with the idea that I had a lot more years ahead of me. Middle age was something I had started thinking about. Not like a mortality thing. More career concerns. I was worried that I wasn't moving up the earnings ladder the way I thought I should have by age thirty-five. Those worries were all irrelevant now. Stupid even, in hindsight.

"So how long have you been alive? You said you were in Paris when the walls came down."

"The Germans. They surrounded the city. Cut it off. People were eating flowers. And horses."

"Was this like the Nazis and stuff like that?" I had only a basic cable education in history.

"Not those pigs. It was before that. Before cars and streetlights. Before I became as you see me."

"Some German turned you?"

"No. The cannons and bombs fell on the city. They drove a tribe from their lair. They came to my parent's house looking for a place to hide. And feed."

Her nails scraped furrows over my chest as she spoke.

"They turned me. I joined them. When the city fell and the Germans came in, we left Paris. Those were hard days. I left the tribe after that. I have been on my own."

"All that time?" I said.

"There were others I hunted with. Never for long."

I wondered how long I had.

We lay entwined like that until the sun, unseen from our shelter, came up. Not speaking. Not moving. I felt Roxanne go limp against me. The dark blanket of sleep fell over me. Before I surrendered to it I spoke to her.

"Can you do something for me?"

"What is it?" she said. Her tongue was heavy.

"Can you stop calling me *mon petit*?"

I felt her cheek rise into a smile where her face rested on my chest.

"What about '*mon chaton*'?" she said.

"What does that mean?" I said.

"My lover," she said. Her voice faded away. She nestled against me.

"Sounds good." I sank into a darkness sweet and deep.

Of course, it was just another one of her lies.

• 11 •

We had enough blood in the kitchen fridge to see us through another night.

Since we didn't have to hunt we spent the evening in. I channel surfed on the big screen in the living room. Roxanne couldn't sit still.

"You need to move the car," she said.

Nothing on the TV was interesting me anyway. It all seemed shallow and unreal now. With immortality to look forward to, the problems of all those people on television seemed more trivial than ever.

I drove the Impala to a parking lot next to the community tennis courts and left it there. I walked back past houses either dark or lit by the shuddering blue light of TVs. A pair of late night joggers passed me. A man and woman. Earbuds in place. Fluorescent strips glowed on their windbreakers. Little reflective strips on their sneakers flashing as they bounced along. The man raised a hand and nodded a greeting.

"Nice night," I said.

They trotted by me. I could smell their sweat, taste the salty tang of it on my tongue. Their elevated heart rates beat in my ears. I turned, stopping by the curb to watch them move around the curve of the street until they were out of sight. I was full, satisfied, by my meal of hospital blood. But there was still a stir of desire as I watched the joggers move away into the night.

They'd never know how close they came. I was a thing to fear. I was a thing that made the dark frightening.

That made me dangerous.

That made me a monster.

I came back to the house already in a bad mood to find Roxanne climbing the walls. We argued over whether to stay or go. It got hot. She threw a Rent-A-Center lamp at me. It shattered against the fireplace mantel, sending plaster everywhere. She stormed off to somewhere in the house. I let her.

By dawn she hadn't returned and I lay in the big queen bed alone until the hammer of sleep dropped on me and I was out for the day.

I have no idea what roused me. The scrape of a key in the lock. A shuffle of soles over hardwood floors.

My eyes opened and I jerked up on one elbow.

There were voices from downstairs. One boomed up to me louder than the others.

"And then we'll check out the bedrooms."

• 12 •

It wasn't like waking from the deep sleep. The closest I can describe it is coming around after anesthesia. I remember waking up after getting my wisdom teeth out. My mother by the bed, patting my hand and speaking my name. I wanted nothing more than to sink back into the cotton candy dreamland the drugs had taken me to.

This was like that, only deeper somehow. It took all I had to roll out of the bed and stumble to the door. I fought the need to lie down with every step. My eyelids felt like they were being drawn down by hundred pound weights. The whole world was canted to one side. The door to the bedroom seemed to get farther away not closer.

I made it to the hall and slid along with my back to a wall to hold myself up. The voices rose up from the foyer, echoing in the two-story open space.

"All the appliances are included. And the central air was replaced just last year."

"What about the home association fee?"

"It's quarterly at three-oh-five. That includes your cable. And you saw those tennis courts, right?"

I wanted to look for Roxanne. I had no idea where she was or even if she was still in the house.

"Jesus!"

They'd found the smashed lamp in the living room. They'd find the blood packs in the Sub-Zero next. I couldn't remember if I'd wiped the blood drops off the kitchen counter.

"I'm terribly sorry. This has never happened before."

"Well, we're not staying here. There could still be someone here."

"You're right. Let's go back to my car."

I heard the beep of a cell phone being tabbed. Three beeps. 911. The babble of voices faded as they exited the house. The front door slammed with enough force to be felt through the carpet under my bare feet.

I ran from door to door calling for Roxanne in a stage whisper. No answer.

Like I said, we'd drawn the blinds and drapes in every room. Still, muted sunlight came through the windows and around the gaps in the treatments. It was enough to add a queasiness to the stupor I was already in. Bedrooms, baths and a bonus room. All empty. Roxanne had either found a hiding place already or was long gone.

I lost track of time in my search. I stood at the top of the stairs, steadying myself with a hand to the newel post. I steeled myself for the climb down the steps to the first floor. The staircase swung like a rope bridge in a high wind. There was more sunshine leaking in on the first floor through the windows either side of the front doors. The sliders in the kitchen had no blinds. I'd be unprotected against the light down there. I had to find Roxanne before anyone else came in.

The front door opened. I stepped back into the relative gloom of the second floor. Two cops came into the foyer. Their hands were empty but their tread was wary, their manner tense. Their heartbeats were racing though their voices were level. One stood by the open door with a hand resting on the butt of his holstered weapon. Blinding afternoon glare sprayed in behind him. I covered my face with my hands and backed away toward the bedrooms. The other cop moved into the house, calling out that a police presence was here and anyone in the house had to make themselves known now. The click of light switches being flipped.

As quiet as I could I made my way back to the master bedroom. I thought about the closet. I thought about locking myself in the bathroom. Even in my muddled state I rejected those hiding places.

The calling voices of both cops came closer. They were climbing the stairs, blocking any chance of escape. Like I could leave the house in broad daylight. Floorboards creaked in the hallway.

I dropped to the carpet and rolled under the bed. The dust ruffle dropped down behind me. I lay on my back with my head turned to watch the open door.

Somewhere doors opened and closed. The section of hall I could see from under the bed grew brighter as blinds were pulled and drapes parted. A pair of polished brogans came into view to step into the room.

"The hell?"

The shoes moved across the carpet faster now. A ripping sound as the duct tape came away. Sunshine blasted in creating a rectangle of fire coming through the gap between the bottom of the ruffle and the carpet. I shrank in from the sides of the bed to the center. My eyes were pressed tight. I could still feel the sickening glow touching the bare skin of my arms and face. I suppressed the moan trying to rise up my throat.

Both cops were in the room now. I couldn't follow what they were saying to one another. The radiance all around was beginning to sear at my skin. Their voices were excited. They pounded around the room pulling closets open. I could hear rubber soles squeaking on bathroom tile. The shower curtain rings clinked as one of them searched the tub.

They stood at the foot of the bed talking. I tried to hold my breath until I remembered that I had no breath to hold. A radio crackled. They exited the room at a run. Feet on the stairs. The front door slamming shut.

I lay there in the sudden silence roiling in the furnace heat washing over me. The hair on my arms crinkled and turned to gray ash. It felt like the flesh was shrinking on my bones. If I stayed here any longer the cops would find a pile of charcoal when they came back.

I had to get out of the light. I crawled on my belly from under the bed on the side opposite the uncovered windows. With my fingers clawing I pulled myself toward the walk-in closet. The cops had left the folding doors open. Crossing the bars of sunlight between me and the sheltering dark inside the closet was agony. Each beam felt like a scalding whip across my back.

I made it to the closet and rose on one knee to pull the accordion door closed. There was a painful bar of light coming through the gap under the door. I pulled my t-shirt off and stuffed it as best I could across the foot of the doorway.

I crept into the deeper dark at the back of the closet and curled up in a ball in a far corner. My whole body stung as though I'd been flayed from head to foot. The enclosed place filled with the stink of burned hair. My arms were ashen black. My face was probably the same.

The cops would be back and they'd find me here. This would look like more than just simple vandalism. The blood packs in the fridge and the kitchen trashcan made sure of that. They'd find me. And they'd find Roxanne if she was still here.

There wasn't a damned thing I could do about it. I huddled in the dark and gave in to the utter exhaustion that was drawing me to oblivion. Within seconds the burning pain was gone. I slipped away into restful senselessness.

• 13 •

Roxanne was dragging me across the yard behind the house. I don't remember her pulling me from the closet or the house. We were out in the dark of the backyards. She was helping me around swing sets, pool fences and picnic tables.

"Walk, damn you," she said.

I found my feet and managed a stumbling gait. She gripped my wrist and led me away between the houses. It was full dark now. A healing dark. My skin still burned from the sun, but the searing pain had faded in intensity to a kind of constant tingle. I went to scratch at my arm and Roxanne batted my hand aside.

"You'll make it worse," she hissed.

"We have to get to the car," I said.

"They took the car away. There is no car."

We came to the end of the block. She took the lead, moving at a crouch between houses. She waved me ahead and together we crossed the street and into the shadows between houses across the block.

"I can't make it any further," I said. I collapsed against a central air housing.

"You stay and you will be found. You're not dying, only weak from hunger. You have to feed." She took a grip on my hair and yanked me upright.

Roxanne had fed. I could smell it on her. A thick beefy smell. The blazing heat of want built in my gut. My tongue flicked over my lips.

"I'm hungry, Roxanne," I said. It came out wheedling like a spoiled child.

"First we get a car. We have to get far from here."

My mind was muddled, confused. I sensed an urgency close to fear in her voice.

The next block of houses backed onto a wooded section. We tramped together over the uneven ground and across a runoff stream, startling some deer watering there. The strand of woods ended at a two-lane road. Keeping to the shadows of the trees we followed the road to an intersection where a group of businesses were clumped on each corner. A Walgreen's, a tire store, a BK and a gas station with a food mart. We crouched behind a hedge that ran along the back lot of the food mart behind the dumpsters.

"We need to steal a new car," she said.

"I don't know how to do that," I said.

"You can't steal a car?"

"Can you?"

"I'm not a criminal."

I almost laughed at that until I felt her hand on my arm clamping down hard.

"There," she pointed.

An SUV had pulled up to the pumps in front of the food mart. A guy in sweats popped out from behind the wheel and hustled toward the store. White vapor spilled from the exhaust. The SUV was running. That meant the keys were in it. It also meant that there was probably at least one passenger still in the car.

Roxanne shoved me forward. She kept shoving until we were at the gas pumps. I crept around the driver's side and reached the door in time to see Roxanne pulling a shouting woman out the passenger side door. The woman swung a fist that Roxanne slipped away from. Roxanne whipped the woman's face with an open slap that sent the woman reeling between the pump islands. She came down hard on her ass with a squeak.

"Get in. Drive." Roxanne slid into the seat.

I got behind the wheel, popped us into gear and went screaming off the lot to make a lurching left through a yellow light. I floored it down the two-lane we'd come up.

The trees and houses gave way to open fields either side of the road. I recognized the road we were on. It was a surface road that joined a wider boulevard that led east to the interstate. The world was shimmering blue under a half moon. The only lights visible were the occasional farm houses set way back off the road. We passed a few cars coming the other way. The headlights were like onrushing comets that blinded me. Roxanne found a pair of sunglasses up on the visor and slid them onto my nose. They helped to cut down the glare if not the piercing pain of the headlight beams.

I was weak and dazed. It was a fight to keep on the right side of the white line snaking toward us out of the dark.

"I don't feel right," I said.

"You'll be fine when you feed. You'll heal. Everything will be all right," she said.

"How did you get me out of there? Where were you today?"

"I found a place in the attic over the garage as you should have done."

"But the police. Why didn't they find me?"

"They did not come back for a long time. I watched them tow your car away."

"They weren't watching the house?"

She made a huffing sound.

"You think the world is like a detective story. You believe the police turn out in droves over someone breaking into an empty house?" she said. I wasn't sure if she was mocking me or the police.

"The blood in the refrigerator."

"There are all kinds of sick people in the world. They are not looking for us, *mon petit.*"

"You promised not to call me that anymore."

"*Je suis désolé, mon chaton,*" she said. It came out as an exaggerated coo. It *was* me she was making fun of.

"You fed. I can smell it on you. You smell like takeout cheeseburgers." The ball of flame in my stomach licked higher.

"So, I fed." She shrugged.

"That's why you're in such a hurry to get away. What did you do?"

"I fed." She looked away toward the utility poles flashing past.

"Damn it," I said. I hit the wheel with the heel of my hand.

We merged onto the boulevard lying bilious yellow under halogen lamps. I could see the glow of the interstate overpass ahead of us. We'd be up the ramp and gone within minutes.

The blooping noise behind us repeated twice before a siren's wail started up. A galaxy of red and blue lights washed over us. Strobing high beams stabbed at my eyes from the rear view mirror. I turned to look behind. Two city police cars were racing one another toward our back bumper.

· 14 ·

"Drive faster," Roxanne said.

"In this piece of shit?" I looked at the dash. The needle was bobbing over empty. We should have waited until they filled up.

The cop cars were pulling up on us, horns honking along with the droning sirens. They'd have us boxed before I could make the onramp.

"They can't catch us," she said. She was turned in the seat to look back. The crazed lights played over her eyes, making them glow red then blue then red again.

"What can they do to us? Shoot us? We're dead already," I said. My foot was to the floor. The wheel wobbled and juddered under my hands.

"Have you ever been shot? It hurts," she said. She looked at me, mouth twisted in fury.

I remembered that puckered scar on her spine.

We were both thrust forward. One of the cop cars tapped our rear with its bull bar. The second one crept up my side of the SUV. They were setting up for a pit move to drive us against the guardrail. I slew sideways and caught the cop car along the side. It swerved onto the medium, churning up rooster tails of dirt and grass. It revved and crossed in front of us at an angle. The cop behind us slammed into our rear again. Metal shrieked. I saw sparks dancing in the rearview.

Roxanne reached across me and grabbed the wheel in both hands. She wrenched it hard to the right. The back end flew out and we skidded over the gravel of the verge to slam hard into the steel guard rail.

Our speed carried us over the rail. For a few seconds we were airborne. I turned the wheel in an impotent attempt to keep us level. No good. We tilted to one side to come down sliding on a grassy slope. The airbags exploded. Beads of glass flew at me. I was punched in the face hard. My skull rocked back, sending the headrest flying. We came to rest on the passenger side, the engine still hammering, my foot still jammed to the floor. Back wheels spinning in the air, spraying mud.

I was dazed for a moment. The engine died to idle then choked itself out. I came around to find myself half-in, half-out of the driver side window, covered in gritty powder off the steering column airbag.

Voices came down from above. Cops slipping, sliding and cursing down into the ditch where we lay.

"Did someone call for an ambulance?"

"Hector's on the horn now."

"I got one here. The driver. Get around the other side."

"Anyone with him?"

"There was a girl I think."

"Don't see her now."

"Sure as hell she didn't run off from this."

Flashlights played over me. I closed my eyes to cut out the glare. The world went pink and streaked through my eyelids. I felt a rough hand grab my arm and hold it, fingers pressed on my wrist.

"This one's dead."

"I don't see any blood."

"No pulse and he's not breathing. That's dead in my book."

"That's not our call. That's the EMTs' problem."

I opened my eyes a slit. Two cops were close in. A redheaded cop with a weightlifter's build stood on the slope squinting.

"He's by himself. Didn't you say you saw a girl, Chad?"

"Thought I did. I'm going to look for her." The redheaded cop. He moved out my sight.

The other two cops stepped away. One of them cursing as his foot went into the water at the bottom of the gully. I considered running, only I wasn't sure where I was. Roxanne took off on me. Must have been less than a second after we came to a stop. Or maybe she was thrown. The cop went looking for her. She could be in the surrounding darkness watching us.

The hunger was gnawing at my insides even more fiercely than before. A weakness, a crushing fatigue, came over me. I couldn't run. I probably couldn't even stand up. I needed to feed.

The ambulance came and along with it two EMTs who cursed a bitter blue streak at having to bring a gurney down the slick muddy surface to the bottom of the gully then haul me up to where their rig sat. One of the cops offered to follow the ambulance to the hospital. They'd need to ID me.

"Look at this son of a bitch," an EMT said when they had me up under the highway lights.

"Thought he was a black guy. But he's just a black white guy. What's with his skin?" the other said.

"That's one sunburnt motherfucker," a cop said. He snorted. I felt him lean close to rifle my pockets.

I listened to him go through my wallet, flicking through credit cards.

"He's local. I *guess* that's him in the license photo." He smelled like aftershave and mustard. And blood. I could smell the sweet, sticky, caramel apple smell of his blood moving through his veins. The lure of it came off him like heat off a furnace. I fought down the urge to spring at him. In my condition I had no chance against a half dozen guys.

I'd have to ride this one out. Ride it all the way.

* * *

With a series of bumps the EMTs rolled me into the ER. I had my eyes locked open now, unmoving and staring. An ER doc gave me a once over and pronounced me to be deader than shit. A nurse snapped a bracelet with a bar code around my wrist. I was parked in a curtained alcove until someone could come to wheel me away. Sounds came through the curtains. The place was hopping. Docs and nurses jogging past. Some drunk was arguing with someone who kept telling him to calm his ass down. A baby was crying. A doctor called out for a blood panel. I wasn't sure what that was. It sounded delicious.

A guy in stained baby blue scrubs came along and kicked the brakes from under my cart to wheel me away to the elevators. He smelled like garlic and vinegar and a faint whiff of cannabis. Earbuds dangled from his breast pocket. He pulled the sheet up over me and got me into the elevator with a series of jarring impacts. I could hear him humming to himself along to the music in his ears.

A ding, a clump, a thunk and we were rolling again into a hall. I was parked again along a long wall and the orderly walked away. I stayed that way a while until two more guys came along, read my bracelet and rolled me off onto a loading dock. They spent some time slipping a body bag over me, zipped it tight. The inside of it smelled of Clorox and corruption. I felt myself lifted and set down without much ceremony on a hard metal surface. Doors clunked shut and I was moving again. The back of some kind of vehicle.

I couldn't see a thing, blind inside the bag. The sick feeling that sunlight brought came over me. I resisted the urge to convulse. Direct sunlight couldn't reach me through the thick black vinyl. I wasn't burning. But every second was torture.

The drive was over. The *beep beep beep* of a reverse warning as the vehicle backed to a stop. The doors clanged open and I was lifted up and roughly dumped onto a smooth surface and wheeled off once more.

The foot of the cart banged doors aside and we were in a room that smelled of disinfectant and feces. The guy rolling me said something to someone else in the room.

"You see it last night?" my driver said.

"My girlfriend came over. I DVRed it," the other said.

"You got to *see* it, bruh."

"Uh huh."

A wire was twisted tight around my big toe. My tag.

A heavy latch was undone. Steel on oiled steel rolled to a clanking stop. Together they lifted me from the gurney onto a chilly metal shelf and rolled me into a dark place. The door slammed back into place and I was alone in the frigid dark wrapped like leftovers.

• 15 •

I lay in cold blackness, listening to the muffled conversation of the two orderlies. They were morons and I began to drift off. The sickness brought on by sunlight was gone and I could feel the sleep state come over me.

I'd be helpless for the next twelve hours or so. Especially in my weakened, famished state. I could try popping out of this drawer and overcoming the two stoners. But I just didn't feel it. I tried to weigh the risk of escaping now against the chance that I might be rolled out of my vault and dissected. In the end I was swept under by the pull of sleep. The real dark melted into infinite dark, my senses fading away to nothing.

I woke in silence. Night had come at some point while I slept the long nap. I ran hands over my arms and torso as much as I could in the tight confines of the bag. My clothes were still on. My skin intact. No one had opened my drawer. I was still on the autopsy waiting list. If I still breathed I would have let out a mighty sigh of relief.

No sound reached me from outside the drawer. I listened for a long while before testing the inner surface of the door at my feet through the material of the body bag. I was expecting some kind of latch, handle or press bar. That was stupid. The people stored in these drawers were dead. I remembered a song I heard my grandmother sing a few times.

Why build a wall 'round the graveyard when nobody wants to get in?
Why build a wall 'round the graveyard when nobody can get out?

Excuse me for being pissed off but I hammered at the door with my feet as much as the bag would allow. No one came to check out the pounding noise down in the morgue. The exertion cost me. I lay back limp as a rag to suffer blazing pangs of hunger spinning like a ball of fire in my gut.

No idea how much time had passed before I heard the sound of a swinging door from outside my drawer. A scuffing of rubber soles over tiles. A radio came on. A hand turned the tuning dial from hip-hop through country and came to rest on a talk station. A guy talking about the possible presence of extraterrestrials in the President's cabinet. I knew that was an after-midnight show. I was deep into the night with my hunger clawing holes in me.

I heard the click of a latch and the rumble of a drawer opening. I lay back, willing myself to be still, inert, and even more lifeless than I felt.

Another click and clack and the niche I was in filled with light. I was drawn out under the fluorescents. A guy in full surgical scrubs muscled me onto a rolling cart. He huffed and puffed with the effort and not gently. I was dead, right? He worked an arm under my shoulders and kind of flipped me over onto the cart. I landed face down, striking my head on the metal surface with a meaty crunch. He rolled the cart alongside a steel autopsy table. He pushed me sliding from the cart and onto the convex surface of the cutting board. He levered me onto my back and wheeled the cart back toward the wall of drawers.

To my right a middle-aged woman lay on the next table. She wore sleep pants and a loose t-shirt with a dark blotch of dried blood between her breasts. Her mouth was open in a yawn that would last all eternity. Her eyes stared upward, shining like buttons, into the ceiling lights.

The cart rolled back to my left. The guy grunted as he shoved a heavy set man onto the next table in the row. He moved past me to return to the woman on the slab to my right. I moved my eyes askance to watch him work.

He pulled on a face mask and strapped a clear plastic shield on his head, lowering it to cover his face. First step was cutting away the woman's clothes with a pair of shears. The t-shirt came away with a Velcro sound, the fabric glued to the dried blood from several wounds to her chest. They looked like stab wounds. Once she was naked the guy took a vial of blood using the artery on the inside of a leg for access. The room smelled with the musk of the sweet syrup. He wrote on a pad of stickers, removed one and wrapped it about the vial. I followed his hand as he placed the full vial atop the pile of the woman's shredded clothes. The blood was thick and gooey and left an oily film on the inside of the glass.

I never wanted anything more in my life. I fought down the urge to jump up and help myself. My eyes flicked back to the guy at work. He caught the motion and looked my way, studying me for a long ten seconds before returning to the job at hand.

On the radio the golden-throated host was giving crap to some caller about whether the Secretary of Education was a gray or a green alien.

The guy used a syringe to take fluid samples from one of the woman's eyes. With a longer needle he drew a tube of urine from the bladder. Each of these got a sticker. He set them by the blood vial.

The vials of blood, eye fluid and piss went into a refrigerator at the back of the room. I caught a glimpse of a plastic rack loaded with rows of vials. A fresh gout of flame rose up my throat making it an effort to remain in place.

He sat at a stool by a counter and made notes on a form. Then he folded that form up over the top of the pad before turning to me.

My unfocused and unmoving eyes studied him as he leaned over the table to study me. He had some mileage on him. In his forties maybe, but looked ten years older. Sallow skin and dark circles under his eyes. He sweated a beer smell. More than a day's stubble on his falling jowls. This guy had fallen a long way from med school to wind up a flunky in a public morgue.

He looked at my bracelet and compared it to his clipboard. Then he started at the neck of my t-shirt with the shears. He caught a movement of my eyes and stopped, head canted, to look into my eyes.

I blinked.

"Hey," I said.

• 16 •

His face showed no reaction. It just froze like it was with a comical look of puzzlement that crinkled his brows together. He slipped from view to crash to the floor.

I pushed up off the steel table with some effort. The world seemed very far away. I stepped over the guy's body to stumble to the refrigerator. My hands looked miles away at the end of my arms as I pulled the door open. Inside were the rows of vials, each nestled in the pocket of a plastic tray. Dozens of them.

I pulled a tray out and dropped to the floor in front of the open fridge. The vials were like those little bottles of booze they have on airplanes. I popped one after the other and downed them like tequila shots.

More like Jell-O shots. Chilled and viscous. The gooey mess slid down my throat to douse the burning. I felt the furnace turn to a warm embrace and the delicious heat spread to my arms and legs. My head felt like I was rising from the depths of an icy pool. I broke the surface with a delicious thrill as my senses all rushed back into focus at once.

I had the strength now to clamber up off the tiles and turn out the room lights. The lamp inside the fridge provided more than enough light. I bent over the body of the morgue flunky and placed my ear to his chest. No heartbeat. No breathing. The blood was unmoving in his veins. The guy's heart went when I spoke to him. It was probably due to pop anyway. Tonight turned out to be his night.

The goop in the vials had revived me but it wasn't the same. Roxanne was right about the canned stuff. I needed living blood.

I found a scalpel among a mess of tools that had dropped from a tray when he fell. I made a long slice along his neck and took my fill while the whisky-voiced guy on the radio told me I should consider gold as part of my retirement portfolio.

The feeding left me logy. Like after my first beer back when I was a kid. I'd have liked nothing better than to lie back on the dead guy and take in the glow. Only I knew I had to move. I was already on the ragged edge of any luck that I had. I sat up and unwound the tag off my toe. My shoes and socks were long gone. The dead guy wore knockoff sneakers inside paper booties. I pulled them off. My feet swam in them. I stuffed the booties into the toes and laced them up. Before leaving the room I snatched the trays of blood vials from the fridge and dumped them into a trash bag I took from a waste can I found under the counter.

With my prizes clinking in my arms I slipped out of the morgue and followed a long basement corridor to an exit. There was a bright yellow plaque with dire black letters on it bolted to the door. I ignored it. A fire alarm went off when I pushed the crash bar on the door. A deafening pulsing bleat. The fire door brought me to an outside stairwell. I raced up the concrete steps and through a hedge to run across a lot with a few cars parked well apart from one another.

Restored to full strength by the recent feast, I felt like my feet were flying. I raced into the dark beyond the wavering glare of the parking lot's sodium vapor lamps. A residential neighborhood of older houses, what we called starter homes, lay beyond. I ran between two of them, leaping a privacy fence between two garages, and found a service alley that ran behind the back yards to the ends of the block in either direction. A dog barked somewhere close. A big one. Claws scrabbled at a vinyl fence across the alley. I let out an explosive animal hiss. The scrabbling stopped. The dog's barking dropped to a yelp then silence.

I moved away at a walk then through the humble two-bed/one-baths with my bag of goodies swinging at my leg. The night was alive for me. The stars above shone like beads of glass. I walked the silent blocks between dark houses without a thought for what might come next. I had all eternity to decide that.

But first I needed to find Roxanne.

• 17 •

I guess my stuff, wallet, keys and the rest, were in an evidence bag somewhere in a police station. Or maybe Roxanne was right. I read too many detective stories. My stuff could be in a trash bin. In any case, I was broke and homeless.

No watch so I didn't know what time it was. Something was telling me morning was coming. An inner clock. I needed to find someplace dark where I'd be left alone to wait out the daylight.

Breaking into an empty house was out of the question. I wasn't in the part of town where my listings were located. Very working class this side of the interstate. And so many places were wired these days. I wasn't forgetting Roxanne's warning about entering places uninvited either. She never did tell me what would happen if I tried that.

I passed a fenced lot where school buses were starting their engines. Clouds of exhaust spreading in the cold air. A few were pulling onto the street in all directions to pick sleepy kids off curbs all over the district. That wasn't good. I looked to the sky. Cloudless except for a few vapor trails. It looked a little on the pink side off to what I thought might be the east. I realized if I'd been a more diligent Boy Scout, or a Boy Scout at all, I'd be better at this. Never made it past Webelos.

Panic was setting in. I started to run with no idea where I was running to. There was a kind of park and municipal buildings of some kind. A row of dumpsters along a fence line. I rejected that idea. With my luck today was a pick-up day. And I thought I'd rather die than take a nap in a dumpster. The irony was lost on me. A few blocks later I was thinking my pride could stand spending a day sleeping in garbage. The sky was growing lighter along the horizon. There was no time to run back to the dumpsters. They were blocks behind me. I had the crazy idea that I could just keep moving west. Stay ahead of the sun. If I had a jet maybe.

I was in a parking lot, moving along the rear of a strip mall. There were trucks pulled up at a loading dock behind a store, engines running. Voices came from under the awning that arched over the backs of the semis. I climbed up on the dock. Vendors were rolling carts stacked with boxes through hanging plastic straps and into golden light coming from inside the store. I stood up straight and parted the strips to walk in with as much confidence as I could muster. I tried to look like I belonged.

No one paid the slightest attention to me. A man at a standing steel desk was ticking off items on a manifest while a vendor sipped from a take-out cup. Others were moving around, stacking cartons onto hand trucks. Most had earbuds in place, bobbing heads to music only they could hear.

I snagged a clipboard from a hook and moved deeper into the rows of high metal racks piled with merchandise. No one questions anyone in a hurry with a clipboard in his hand. Not even a scabby, sickly pale, guy in a wrinkled t-shirt and jeans. At least I hoped not.

Pure survival instinct led me to the darkest area of the stock room. I climbed up on a forklift and then up a stack of crated air conditioners to a higher shelf piled with dusty boxes marked "pool toys." They wouldn't be stocking these for sale for months. I crawled in, shoving the bag of clacking vials ahead of me. I lowered myself down on top of the boxes. They sagged a bit under my weight and smelled of mold, dust and plastic. Inches above my face was the wire mesh floor of the next shelf above me.

I closed my eyes and listened to the sounds from below. Voices, the squeak of carts and the banging of swing doors. A whiff of coffee. The world of daylight was starting up as my night was ending. The blinking glare of the overheads didn't reach me in the shadows where I lay.

The deep drug of sleep came crashing down on me. Before I was swept away and under I wondered to myself what the hell I was going to do that night.

And the next. And the next. And the next.

I came awake in full dark. Check that. There was a slight blue glow from somewhere below me. I poked a head out from my hidey-hole to see the stock area was dark except for a few safety lights along the floor. The place was silent.

Hooking the bag over one arm I climbed down to the floor. I crept along in the near dark, my head turning side to side, eyes searching for any movement. The loading dock was shuttered closed, the outside doors rolled down and padlocked. I reached a pair of swing doors that led into the store. No light came through the portholes set in them at eye level. I took a peek through the smeared plastic panes. The store beyond was mostly dark. Can lights high in the ceiling sent down cones of weak amber beams to fall in puddles on the sales floor.

I moved through the doors and across the tiles to follow aisles of bath towels, bed sheets and pillows to the center of the place. A big box discount store. The kind of place that stays open late. I must have slept a long time. After the forty-eight hours I'd just been through I guess I needed it.

But that meant that this would be a short night for me. That troubled me. I could stay in my stockroom hidey-hole another night. That idea didn't appeal to me. I wanted to be moving. I needed to find Roxanne.

At least dinner wasn't going to be a problem. I drained a half dozen of the vials to bring the hunger down to the glow. And I needed a change of clothes and maybe a shower.

I picked out new jeans, some t-shirts, a canvas jacket, work boots. I found a sturdy overnight bag to hold the remaining blood vials and a bag of socks. I got a wallet, comb and a pocket knife. In jewelry I found a wristwatch that was down-market for my tastes but the best they had. I wound up taking a dozen of them in men's and ladies' styles. My taste for larceny aroused, I went to electronics and shoved as many smart phones into the overnight bag as would fit along with a stack of pay-as-you go phone cards.

I thought back to the scalpel I left behind at the morgue.

In hardware I found a carpet knife with a retractable blade. I took an extra pack of blades, too.

At the rear of the store there was a shower in the employees' men's room. I stripped down, stuffing my filthy clothes into a bin. In the shower I scrubbed hard with soap and a washcloth. The layer of scabs left by the sun damage sloughed off to leave clearer skin beneath. Not pink but clear of most of the discoloration left by my near-lethal sun bath. Crisp flakes of dry flesh dotted the swirl of sudsy water at my feet.

By sheer habit I started to comb my hair before the mirror. I stepped away and simply brushed it back off my forehead. I wondered if my hair would keep growing and decided it would not.

In fresh clothes and with a bag of swag over my shoulder I made my way to a fire exit at the rear of the store. I paused before it to check my new watch. It was almost half past midnight. I had six hours or less to either find Roxanne or another safe place to hide myself.

I shoved on the panic bar and the fire alarm shrieked to life. I bolted through it into the night.

• 18 •

Forget all the places you think someone like me might hide. There are no castles here. No empty houses at the end of lonely country roads. No unlocked mausoleums stacked with cozy coffins. Nothing so creepy cool as that.

I spent the next day sleeping in a junkyard. A sprawling place with rows of cars and trucks cannibalized for parts. I slept in a graveyard after all. I climbed the fence and found a Lincoln with a popped trunk lid. It was roomy enough. I climbed in and tied the lid down with a piece of wire.

I stayed hungry through the night, only draining two vials before sleeping. That way I could make my supply last. It didn't do much to cool the fire. The hunger was almost all I could think about. It worked to drive everything else from my mind.

Food was never an issue with me before. As a single guy I ate when I was hungry. Coffee and a bagel for breakfast when I had the time. Lunch was fast food drive-through. Dinner, Chinese or pizza. I ran three times a week and played pick-up hoops games at the park near my condo to maintain my college waist size.

But this new hunger was a whole new thing—an obsession. It was an addiction that was determined to drive me to feed every hour that I was awake.

Feeding wasn't my only problem. My life, my afterlife, was in the shitter. I had no money and no clue of where to get any. My idea of selling the watches and cell phones at a pawn shop went nowhere. I recalled that the phones and minutes cards needed authorization at the register when purchased. They were useless without that. And I'd watched enough pawn shop shows on TV to know that they'd spot the watches as stolen and probably call the cops. I threw the phones down a sewer but kept the watches for possible barter. Beyond that I had no plans other than finding Roxanne.

That presented a whole new list of problems. I had no car and missed it dearly. Walking everywhere was a pain in the ass. And walking alone at night was only going to get me in trouble. I could only cover so much ground in a night. That made it harder to look for Roxanne.

And I needed to find her. Beyond having no one else to relate to, she had all the knowledge I needed. I was a beginner at all this and had way more questions than answers. She'd been doing this for a hundred years or more. She knew how to make this fucked-up lifestyle work. I needed her mentoring.

I sensed that she wasn't looking for me.

No one crushed the Lincoln while I slept. I took that as a positive sign.

After two vials for breakfast I set out to take advantage of a full twelve hours of darkness.

It was raining, a cold steady drizzle. That suited me fine. My clothes got soaked through after an hour's walking. But the rain was cover. The streets were empty. Passing cars paid no attention to a lone guy hiking through the downpour.

I walked back into my old neighborhood. After an hour watching the lot near my building I followed a Korean family through the entry doors into the lobby. They were busy managing armloads of shopping bags. A cute little kid was last in line and held the door for me. His smile faded when he saw my face. I must have looked like shit, wet as a drowned rat and skin the color of putty. I took the stairs as he backed, eyes goggling, into the elevator where his family waited for him.

I expected to find police tape over my door. There wasn't any. I moved fast past Cheryl and Nancy's place. Some kind of dance music loud on their TV. I planted a shoulder to my door and pressed hard. It popped open. I caught it before it could crash against the wall. Once again I was surprised at my own strength. A side effect of my new condition, I guessed.

Condition, hell. More like a curse. Exactly like a curse. I was cursed.

The place looked mostly like I'd left it a few nights ago. Some of the furniture was slightly out of place. Old indents in the carpet mashed there by chair legs. I had the vague sense that someone had been here. A whiff of a strange aftershave. I had an unpleasant momentary thrill that my place might be watched. I shook it off. They'd have followed me up. Or braced me at the door.

Moving around the apartment quickly, I shrugged off my wet clothes and put on dry ones. There was a jar of change in the kitchen. I shoved it into my carry-all. In the bedroom I had an envelope of cash in the bottom of a sock drawer. It was still there. Almost four hundred bucks. Either the cops who searched the place were honest or they didn't do a thorough job looking.

I pulled a raincoat from the closet. A Hugo Boss I bought during a good month last year. Black. I probably looked the part now though the bedroom mirror showed nothing but bedroom.

In the kitchen I scooped ice into a plastic zip bag and set it among the remaining blood vials at the bottom of my carryall.

At the door I stood a while checking the peephole and listening before stepping into the hall. I was down the elevator and to the street without seeing anyone. I found a taxi pulled up to a Dunkin' Donuts a few blocks along. The driver decided I was a junkie and told me to fuck off. I showed him my roll of bills.

I gave him directions and a twenty dollar tip to drop me off on a surface road near where the interstate split. He peeled away, leaving me in the rain before the dark opening that led to the tent city. The place where I first fed on live blood. My hand tested the carpet knife in my raincoat pocket, clicking the blade in and out of the handle. The fire in my belly swirled, stoking hotter.

My hunger made my pace quicker, drawing me along with memories of that first mouthful of salty red broth. My mission here wasn't just because I was thirsty. I wanted to find Roxanne.

I watch a lot of the nature shows on TV. Stuff shot in Africa are my favorites. If they taught me anything it's that predators always return to the richest killing ground.

· 19 ·

I watched the tent village from the shadows behind an overpass support. A generator thumped somewhere sending a column of white exhaust up into the frigid air. A tidy little community these pervs had made for themselves. A few of the tents were lit by the flickering blue light of televisions, the sound drowned out by the constant swoosh of traffic on the highway above. Everything was otherwise still. I crouched, stomach burning, to watch the surface road running between the porta potty and the collection of tents and sheds. Like a lion watching a game trail down to the waterhole.

A few hours passed on my stolen watch. The tents were dark. The last of the TVs shut off. The traffic above was intermittent except for the occasional truck rumbling by. A shape separated itself from the dark between the tents and headed for the surface road. My hand went to the knife in my pocket. I took it out and thumbed the blade out of the handle. The figure, a smallish man, walked onto the roadway, shoulders hunched under a down parka.

I made to move for him and stopped. The sound of shifting gravel. A figure rushed out of the shadows of a support column to the other side of the potty shack. A long black leather coat over a hoodie pulled up to hide its features. A blade in a gloved hand caught a glint from the lights from a passing truck overhead. The figure was on a path to intersect the man in the parka.

I watched as the dark figure slipped up from the blind side of the man in the parka and took him in a chokehold grip. The man's hands jumped to scratch at the arm pinning him. The man's feet kicked as he was dragged into the dark behind the porta potty.

Roxanne.

I raced back up the gravel slope to move around the back of the columns through the deepest gloom. Moving as quietly as I could on the slippery aggregate, I came on Roxanne straddling the still form of the man in the parka. She was rifling his pockets. The blade was nowhere in sight.

"I thought I'd find you here," I said.

The figure whirled to face me. Wide eyes in a dark face. A male face. Some kid. Nineteen maybe. No older than twenty-one anyway. A rat-face with a half-assed attempt at a goatee.

Not Roxanne.

"Who the fuck you?" he said.

"Shit," I said.

"Damn right shit," he said. He rose off the unconscious man. I could see the parka rising and falling. The man was alive.

The kid approached me at fast walk. The blade was in his gloved hand again. Some kind of switchblade with a long, razor sharp needle point. With an animal snarl he closed the distance between us and lunged with the blade.

I watched in slow motion as my hand snaked out and took his wrist. He screamed as I bent the wrist back with a meaty snap. I could feel his pulse through the palm of my hand. The fire rose from my belly. My ears rang with the thunder of his rising heart rate. His fingers sprang open. The knife fell to the gravel.

I pulled him closer, his feet leaving the slope. I brought my knife up and struck deep into the soft flesh of his throat and tore to the left across his windpipe. His scream turned to a wet gurgle. I drove him to the ground with my weight atop him and clamped my mouth to the pumping wound. The hot, rich broth filled my mouth as I swallowed over and over again to take it all.

His body went limp under me. His face was a mask of slack horror, eyes and mouth wide, flesh ashen.

Drowsy from feeding, I stood to look around me. I was covered in the shower from his open vessel. The blood was already turning sticky in the cold air. There was blood sprayed all over the gravel in every direction. The man in the parka was still out cold. I could hear his heartbeat, regular and strong.

With as little effort as picking up a kitten I gripped the kid under the arms and threw him over my shoulder. I charged up the long slope into the dark under the highway overpass. There was a broad flat area of gravel fill under the roadway between huge support columns. It ended at a wall with the hoops of steel ladder rungs set in the surface. I climbed them to the top, the kid draped over my shoulder.

The ladder ended in a concrete shelf that left just enough head room for me to walk under the rows of steel beams supporting the highway overhead. The shelf angled upward and stopped a good twenty feet in. I had to stoop way down to make it to the rear of the shelf. I dropped the kid's dead weight in a corner. There was evidence here that someone had used the place for a home. But not for a long time. There was a flattened refrigerator box and a heap of moldering rags; the remnant of some kind of quilt decorated with once-colorful images of Raggedy Ann.

I went down the ladder to creep back down the slope to the kid's intended victim. His wallet lay by him where the kid dropped it. I left him there to get the carry-all bag I'd left behind a column. I came back and looked over the scene. I picked up the kid's knife and, after figuring out how to draw the blade back into the handle, put it in my pocket.

There was blood all around where I'd brought the kid down. The drops gleamed black on the gravel in the gray light from above. The sun was rising on an overcast day. I was running out of time to find a place to hole up. But I couldn't leave the blood here. The man in the parka might report the mugging. If cops found this much blood they'd want to look around. Maybe even bring dogs. They'd find the body. The blood on the gravel had to go.

One by one I gathered up the pieces of gravel with blood on them.

I licked them clean, every stone.

• 20 •

I still had a lot of questions.

Like, what about the whole "native earth" thing? Was I covered as long as I stayed local?

The place I spent that night sure had plenty of indigenous dirt. And piss. And pigeon crap. I wrapped myself in that filthy Raggedy Ann quilt and crawled into the refrigerator box. I lay there, protected in my own personal cocoon, my belly full and the fire tamped down to a pleasant glow. I drifted off listening for the sound of police sirens. I didn't hear anything but the rumble and hiss of the highway traffic a few feet above my head.

It snowed during the day. I woke up to find the world was silvery white under a quarter moon sky. The body of the kid lay where I left it. It was too cold for it to start smelling. To anyone with a normal sense of smell that is. I could smell the death on him. And the cold silence that comes with the cessation of life.

The snow on the gravel slope had a good six-inch covering over where it was exposed to the sky between the two overpasses. The snow cover was undisturbed. Zero footprints. No one climbed it looking for evidence. Odds were the man in the parka came to, found his wallet next to him, and scuttled back to his tent counting his blessings. Not likely for a registered pervert to call 911 to report a simple assault.

I was still feeling the glow of the feast from the night before. There was a gnawing sensation growing in my gut but it was manageable. I had plenty of vials to take the edge off when I needed to. I dug through the carry-all bag to change out of my clothes. My jeans especially were stiff with clotted blood. I used my undershirt to wipe the worst of the stains off my raincoat. I tossed the clothes into the corner by the dead kid.

When the kid was found they'd find the clothes covered in his DNA. My DNA, too. Or were my genetics the same now? In any case it wouldn't lead the cops anywhere. I was dead, too, remember. And besides, as quick as that kid was to use that knife, I had to assume he had a record. He was no newbie mugger. The cops wouldn't waste much of their time looking into how he died, right?

In fact, I probably saved the man in the parka's life. Never mind that I would have taken it myself if the kid hadn't gotten to him first. I considered that a while and it left me with a hollow feeling. I had no desire to justify myself with any bullshit moral equivocations. I was past that. Right and wrong had no meaning for me. Maybe when my belly was full. Only I knew that when the hunger came on I'd feed on anything. There was no use pretending. No use hanging on to who I was before.

That disturbed me for a fleeting second. But only for that second. I was what I was, no longer as God made me.

Roxanne was right about that.

Roxanne.

I went through the kid's pockets and found a roll with just over a hundred in wrinkled bills and a baggie of jagged yellow rocks. Meth, I guess. I was never a drug user. In another pocket I found a key ring with a remote and car key. The cash and keys went into my pocket. The baggie shoved back in the kid's pocket.

I tossed my carry-all to the snow and climbed down the ladder. I would not be returning. There were cheap motels close enough that would take cash with no question. I'd make sure I budgeted my time to get me there with time to spare before sunup. I'd give Roxanne a few hours to show up before I left.

The shadows behind the column hid me and gave me a clear

view of the RSO camp. Not much activity. A few of the hardier souls gathered around a barrel fire. The generator made a flat growling sound that echoed off the snow. Sometime after midnight a city plow lumbered along the surface road making twin berms of filthy snow and spraying salt behind it.

The only change from the night before was that the pervs visited the porta potty in pairs. The man in the parka must have told his pals. They were taking no chances. I watched the parade of tandem campers trudge across the slick surface road to take turns in the shithouse. The hunger rose in me at the sight of each new couple. I sipped from the vials to keep it manageable. Letting the bloodlust force me to take on two at a time was something I wanted to avoid.

The camp quieted. The barrel fire burned down to a stinking smolder. The firewatchers said their goodnights and were snug in their sleeping bags dreaming of playgrounds and Girl Scouts. The last TV winked off. I rose from my crouch to find a hot sheet joint where I could spend the daylight hours.

A figure stepped from the tents, followed by another. It was the man in the parka. I recognized the faux coyote trim around his hood. Must have had a prostate problem to risk another late-night piss run. He had a larger pal with him. This second guy was in a shiny Gore-Tex coat that made him look like a parade blimp. In addition to his height he carried a ball bat in his gloved hand. I stepped farther back into the shadows to watch.

They shuffled on to the john and the bigger man stood sentry outside, stamping his feet against the cold. I settled down to watch until they finished their business then I'd move on to find a room.

A shadow moved against a column behind the porta potty. A shape, moving low, came around into the street and swooped toward the big man in Gore-Tex. The man saw the movement in time to turn and swing the bat two-handed. The shape ducked inside the arc of the bat and had the man down on the snow with an astonishing speed. Something about the movement, ghost-like and feral.

This time it was Roxanne.

She whipped her razor over the fallen man's throat in one fluid motion. A steaming jet of crimson stained a snow drift. She used the collar of his coat for a grip and burrowed her face into his neck, her shoulders heaving with the effort of draining him of every drop.

The man in the parka exploded from the john, his pants still around his ankles. Roxanne sprang up from the Gore-Tex guy as if on wires. The parka stumbled back slipping on the ice or tripped up by his own pants. Roxanne closed the distance between them in a heartbeat. She took his face in her splayed hand and drove it hard against the icy curb. The man in the parka moved no more.

I was a half-step from the edge of the shadows when Roxanne looked up. Her eyes shone yellow but she wasn't looking at me.

A cop car was crunching along the road, its headlights trapping Roxanne and her two fresh victims like actors on a stage.

• 21 •

I waited, watching, for Roxanne to take off. I was ready to follow whichever way she ran. Instead, she stood waiting for the cop car to pull level with her. The driver door opened and a big cop stepped out onto the salted road.

It was the redheaded cop. The guy with the gym muscle. The one who was there when I crashed the car. He stooped to cuff the man in the parka while Roxanne opened the rear door of the cop car to toss in Gore-Tex like a sack of groceries. The cop hefted the smaller man and stuffed him into the rear.

A group of pervs left their tents to stand along the curb watching. The cop waved them away before getting behind the wheel. Roxanne slid in on the passenger side and then they were away. Everyone went back to their tents.

I made a mental note of the cop car's number. Two-Two-Five. It was a county sheriff's car not a city car. It was black and tan and marked with a star on the door. I'd know it again if I saw it.

I gave it a few minutes and moved closer to the porta potty. The salty slush was disturbed by the brief struggle. A pink stain spread across the snow where Roxanne's razor slash had sent the gout of hot blood. I crouched and took a bit of the blood infused snow and popped it in my mouth. It was diluted but still tasted of copper and grease.

There was a thicker puddle at the curb where the man in the parka struck his head. It was congealing in the snow melt, tangy with rock salt. I dipped my fingers in it and sucked the juice from them.

* * *

I walked a few blocks north to where the registered sex offenders from the camp parked their cars. They lined them up along either side of a street running between the interstate fence and the rear of a big brick building. A derelict factory or warehouse. The street was unplowed. The cars were covered in snow.

A shiny red Hyundai mounded over with snow was parked with two wheels up on the curb. I pressed the lock key on the remote I took off the mugger. The headlights of the Hyundai blinked yellow. The car chirruped.

The interior was clean. Nothing on the seats or dash. The kid had no respect for the lives of others but was a neat freak about his ride.

I cranked the key and the engine coughed to life followed by a deafening rumble from behind me. I found the controls for the stereo and turned the music off. The throbbing woofers in the trunk went silent.

I had time to think over what happened on the drive to the golden mile down at the next highway exit.

That cop had chased after Roxanne on the night of the crash. She let him follow her until she could spring an ambush far enough from the road. I didn't know if she turned him or had him under some kind of spell. I didn't even know if that was a thing, that hypnotic deal I saw in movies. She sure didn't use it the night we met. Free-flowing booze and a generous view of her tits were enough to lead to my downfall.

So she had a new partner. One that could provide protective cover. The perfect mate for hunting. I wasn't sure if that would make it harder or easier to find her.

I couldn't help but feel jealous. We didn't have that kind of relationship, Roxanne and I. I'm not even sure how you'd define our relationship. We weren't friends. I think she saw me as a curiosity, an amusement. I saw her as a guide to this new world she'd brought me, unwillingly, into. I still needed her for that. The lessons were not over. I needed someone to show me how this was supposed to work; how I was supposed to survive.

The first motel I came to was just the kind of place I was looking for. The Tartan Motor Lodge. A grinning cartoon Scotsman winked at me from the road sign. An L-shaped structure with two dozen rooms on two levels. It shared a lot with an all-night liquor store and a Denny's. A few cars were pulled up to rooms. Most backed into spots on the freshly plowed lot. Cheaters.

The office was muggy from a space heater humming in a corner. There was a white guy in a wrinkled raincoat registering at the desk when I entered the office. His "date", a heavily made up black woman, stood outside in the cold smoking a Kool and hugging a faux rabbit jacket around her shoulders. Romeo counted out bills and shoved them through the slot in the screen to a weedy looking guy behind a counter.

"You need anything sent over? Drinks? Beer maybe?" the counter guy said.

"We're fine," the raincoat said. He smelled like he'd had enough already. He snapped up the room key from the slot and shouldered past me into the cold.

"How much for two nights?" I said.

"There's a Radisson up the road," the counter guy said after scanning what passed for a lobby to see that I was alone.

"This place is fine."

"Sure. One fifty if you're using a card. One twenty cash."

"And I won't need housekeeping. I just want to sleep."

He took a second look at me. Sized me up for a junkie, which was okay with me.

"Sure. Sure. Hang a sign on the knob."

"Can you pass the word to the maids just to make sure? I'm a sound sleeper."

"Sure. Sure."

I counted out bills, got the key and went up to B-9.

It was about what I expected. A sagging queen bed. Scuffed nightstand and dresser. A cheap TV mounted to the wall. The picture window covered in gold polyester drapes. I shot the bolt home and placed the chain in the loop. To make sure I pushed the dresser against the door. I pulled the mattress off the bed frame and onto the floor. Then dragged the box spring to prop it against the window to block out the light coming off the parking lot. I used sheets and a blanket to jam around the box spring to cut off every chink of illumination. The room was pitch black. I lay down atop the mattress and snapped on the TV.

I surfed around the channels, sipping a few vials of blood while waiting for dawn and the deep sleep that came with it. Twice around the horn brought me back to a local news channel and a story of the police dealing with a baffling mystery of a murder and a missing corpse. I was about to switch back to a poker tournament when a familiar face came on the screen.

Me.

It was my official picture from Handley-Barker. Me wearing my company blazer and friendliest grin. The murder victim was a county medical examiner. Turned out that I was the missing corpse.

My mind was getting fuzzy. Somewhere out beyond my barricaded window and door the sun was coming up. I had to listen hard to the TV to make sense of it; to relate it to what I experienced. The police were on the lookout for the person or persons unknown who killed a county employee while in the commission of snatching of my body. Not a lot of details other than no surveillance video existed of the perpetrators. Of course not. I was the perpetrator. The missing corpse walked out on its own past all their cameras.

The report ended with them saying that the police were looking into my background for any connections that might shed light on what happened.

Good luck with that.

I snapped off the TV and lay back on the mattress and covered up head to toe with a bed cover.

As I fell into drowsiness I made plans for the next night. I ran through my options for finding Roxanne again and came up with nothing. I had to find her. I wasn't going to make it like this. Living day to day. Or night to night. Then my thoughts drifted back to the clerk in the motel office. How he looked at me. I was a junkie to his eyes. And that's what I was now.

Just another addict.

· 22 ·

A Malaysian plane vanished somewhere over the Pacific and wiped every other story off the news cycle. Even the local news channel wasn't covering the mystery of the missing corpse any longer. Part of that could have been that there were no new developments. Certainly no video.

I sat on the edge of the reassembled bed with the remote in my hand, sipping a breakfast dose from one of my last dozen vials. It was thick and a little funky. I should have found a way to keep it better chilled. Lesson learned.

The news the night before presented more questions than it answered. No mention of a missing policeman or police car. The redheaded cop was Roxanne's new playmate. That meant he was turned. That he wasn't listed as missing meant that he was still reporting for work. That made no sense though. How was he able to leave his patrol area to come into the city to hunt with Roxanne? Someone should have noticed that. But what did I know? Maybe county deputies were free roaming agents.

I left the room as I found it and walked across the dark lot to where I left the Hyundai. A cold rain was turning the snow to slush. I pulled out past the Denny's to point the car toward the surface road that ran along the interstate. I stopped and gassed up, paying from the roll of cash I took off the kid.

Roxanne and her cop buddy would be hungry again. I know I was. The RSO camp was easy pickings. Irresistible. I figured to cruise the camp and surrounding streets to look for the cop car. I drove around in an ever widening grid. There were homeless occupying alleys in makeshift sheds of corrugated metal sheets and cardboard. Some sat sharing bottles on stoops of boarded up row houses. This was a hunting ground of the forgotten.

I found the cop's car after a few hours of drifting along the dark streets. Car 225 was pulled up along a fence that ran around a schoolyard. Lights out and engine cold. Footprints in the slush led from the car to the high fence. They continued across the undisturbed snow that blanketed the school yard. Waffle stomper prints from the soles of a large man's shoe. The smaller triangular imprint of cowboy boots. Roxanne's boots.

I pulled the Hyundai around the corner and left it in the shadows between two U-Hauls on the lot of a rental place. I walked back to the fence and scaled the ten feet of links to drop onto the other side. I was careful to skirt the edges of the fence, not disturbing the virgin snow around the twin set of footprints.

The school building was an ancient pile of bricks with a row of prefab schoolrooms set to one side of the lot. A rhythmic *ping-ping-ping* sound came from behind the prefabs. I moved low between them toward the source of the sound. The pinging stopped. It was followed by something striking a surface then the pinging resumed.

Under the light of a pole lamp was an outdoor basketball court surrounded by the walls of the old school building. Roxanne crouched at center court over a body lying prone. A second body lay still near the foul line. The cop was at the far net, dribbling the ball and taking practice shots at the hoop while Roxanne fed.

I watched from the shadows between two prefabs. Roxanne sat back on her heels, her mouth a crimson smear. I backed farther into the shadows to make my way back across the schoolyard and over the fence the way I came.

From where I left the Hyundai I could see the cop car parked by the fence. Roxanne and the cop came into view around the school building. The cop had one body over each shoulder.

Roxanne was up and over the fence like a cat. She stood waiting while, one after the other, the cop held each body over his head and lobbed them over the top of the fence. They landed in the snow, spent and broken things. Roxanne opened the trunk and the cop joined her to stuff the bodies inside. A pair of kids in colorful jackets and bright white sneakers. They'd never go home again. Gangs would get the blame probably.

Back in the car, they pulled from the curb and made a left. I gave them some time and followed, lights out. The streets were empty making the cop car easy to follow even at the two block distance I kept between us. I pulled to a stop when the cop made a right onto a road that turned to cross a steel bridge over the river. The lights of the cop car came to a stop mid span. After a moment or two a pair of dark shapes dropped from the bridge. They dropped into the slowly moving water with a pair of silent splashes. The cop car was on the move again and I followed at a discreet distance.

It was easier to keep up once the cop left the empty streets and turned into denser traffic along one of the avenues. I was able to pull up closer, keeping cars between us all the time. We drove west for a while past brightly lit strips of storefronts between blocks of dark apartment rows. I followed through several turns, falling back as traffic thinned when city turned into county. They pulled into a driveway between rows of naked trees to enter a broad parking area of fifty acres or more surrounding a row of apartment towers. I followed them onto the lot and took a spot along the tree line.

The cop drove into an angled space under a sputtering street pole lamp. Together he and Roxanne walked over the lot to the nearest building and disappeared inside.

I drove around the building a few times, looking up at the windows. It was after one in the morning but still most apartments showed some lamplight from inside. All but the sixth floor, north east corner. The windows there were pitch black.

I knew where to find them now. I drove back to the Tartan to drain the last of my vials and lie dormant until night fell again.

· 23 ·

The world shrank down to my need to feed.

I woke up ravenous. There's no other way to describe it. Obsessed.

The night before, while following the cop and Roxanne, I passed plenty of corners where obvious drug sales were being made. Young men standing idle before shuttered stores. Cars pulled up to the curb, stopping a few seconds before pulling away.

I traced my way back and found a market open for business. Three kids in hoodies and layers of winter clothing waiting to service cars driven in from the suburbs. Nice cars. Recent SUVs and sedans dusted white with salt melt. There was walk-up trade, too. They didn't interest me.

A dark blue Yukon drew my attention. Fat tires, tinted windows. It came to a stop in front of the corner store still open. One of the kids stepped from the flickering neon of the beer signs in the window to lean in the passenger window. The driver reached over the seats holding out bills. The kid counted them and jerked his head, gesturing around the corner. The Yukon pulled into the darker cross street where another kid ran out to him and passed something to the driver.

I followed the Yukon as it made turns to head back to a boulevard lined with strip malls either side. The driver parked in the dark behind an IHOP, engine idling. I pulled up a few spaces away and cut my lights. I stepped out and came around the back of the Yukon. It had those stick figures on the back window. A wife. A husband. Three kids and a dog. There was a COEXIST bumper sticker on the tailgate.

The dark window was rolled up and fogged with condensation inside. I tapped on the glass. A muffled voice from inside.

"I need you to roll down your window." I tried to sound as authoritative as I could. I was afraid the driver would hear the longing in my voice.

A thin guy with horn-rimmed glasses peeped at me over the gap made when the glass rolled down halfway. I could see he had a sweater rolled up to bare his right arm. No other sign of the dope he just bought. He'd have whisked that out of sight in his panic when I knocked on the window.

"All the way please, sir." I used that tone of forced politeness I'd heard cops use on me whenever I got pulled over.

He stabbed a button on the door and the window whirred open. His eyes were on me the whole time. I could see fear there. Hunger too. Like mine.

The driver began to say something. I cut him off with a hand over his mouth and nose. I plunged the tip of the carpet knife into the side of his throat and pulled it across his Adam's apple with a single tug. His hands leapt to his throat and I batted them away to clap my mouth over the wound.

I smelled his rancid sweat through the wool of his sweater. I heard his pulse slowing in my ears even as the font of blood in my mouth slowed. I grabbed his wrist to keep his hand off the car horn. His struggles grew feeble then stopped all together. His skin looked like paper, pale and thin. A tear froze on his cheek.

He was dead. He was empty.

I lifted my head from the white lips of the wound and caught a glimpse of color in the back seat.

A kid asleep in a car seat. I'm not good at ages. A toddler I guess, gently snoring away while Daddy shot up.

There was a smart phone on the seat by the dead guy. It lay

under a newspaper meant to conceal the syringe, lighter, spoon and the tiny white packet that lay there as well. I picked it up and went back to the Hyundai.

I called 911 when I was a few miles away. I gave the dispatcher the location. Told her there was a baby crying in the back of an SUV behind the pancake place. I hung up in the middle of her next question. I rolled the window down and tossed the phone into a lake of slush at the curb.

The cop car was gone from its parking spot. They were out for the night. Frustrated, I punched the dash, putting a permanent dent in the upholstery. In my mind I would brace them on their way out of the apartment building. The plan didn't go much further than that.

I found a spot near the main entrance and parked the Hyundai. It was a secured building. I'd need a key card to run through the slot. The door into the lobby only opened when an occupant buzzed down from their place. I loitered by the wall of mailboxes until a couple of men came in with plastic Target bags hanging from the fingers of both hands. They groused at one another until one of them slid his card down the slot. I moved away from the mailboxes with an apology and held the door open for them and they hustled in. I followed behind as they went to the bank of three elevators. I made for a door off the lobby into a stairwell.

The sterile hallway that bisected the sixth floor ended with a floor to ceiling window that offered a view of the twinkling lights of a highway. There were doors to apartments on either side of the hall. I pressed the bell to the north-east corner unit. I was pressing an ear to the door to listen when I heard the snap of the deadbolt and the door was yanked inward.

Roxanne stood in the door, wearing an open men's dress shirt and panties. Her head bobbed back in a gesture of surprise though her black eyes remained cold.

"What the fuck do you want?" she said.

You know, I wasn't sure.

· 24 ·

"Are you going to invite me in?" I said.

She stood aside and waved an arm at the dark interior. I stepped inside. The place was an open plan with a wide living room and kitchenette off to one side. The windows were covered over with thick plastic trash bags and duct tape. A TV was on in the living room.

"You can't stay," she said.

"Your boyfriend's coming back?"

She slammed the door with a huff and walked to an overstuffed sofa. I followed. She threw herself down, bare feet propped on an arm. She pretended interest in an old movie on the TV.

"Why aren't you out with him?"

"He was called to work."

"You left me, Roxanne," I said. I leaned on the arm of a leather recliner.

"How could I leave you? I was never with you." Her eyes on the TV, a couple seated at a table in a night club while waiters rushed by with trays of drinks.

"You know what I mean."

She shrugged, her lower lip stuck out in a pout.

"We're leaving. Me and him," she said.

"Leaving? For where?"

"They're moving Chad to day shift. We can't stay. Spring is coming anyway. The nights are getting shorter."

Chad.

"Where will you go?"

"I don't know."

"Can I go with you? I can't stay here either."

She laughed at that. A bitter snort.

"I know. I have seen your stupid face on the television. You drew attention to yourself."

"I want to leave, too."

"They are looking for a dead man. No one is looking for you. You are dead. Forgotten."

"Aren't you feeding tonight?"

She rose from the sofa and went into the kitchenette. She came back from the fridge with a plastic baggie of blood. She tossed it to me. It was frosty cold in my hands.

"Chad took them from an ambulance the other night. Help yourself. We have enough," she said. She dropped onto her belly on the couch again.

"Take-out," I said. I slid the packet into a pocket of my raincoat.

She seemed to forget me, watching the TV as the same couple as before ran laughing down a street under a pouring rain. They stepped under the awning before a store to share a gentle kiss.

"I need your help, Roxanne. I'm not good at this," I said.

"You seem to be managing, *mon petit*," she said. We were back to that.

"Not for the long run. I don't know about so many things. I need your experience."

She sighed and turned to me, black eyes blinking.

"I should have known you'd be trouble."

"Well, you got me into this shit." I was getting frustrated.

"You are welcome."

"For what?"

"Immortality."

"Like this? As a junkie? A bottom-feeding parasite?"

She sat up then, running her nails through her hair.

"All right. It is okay. You can go with us," she said.

"What does Chad have to say about that?"

"He will do as I tell him to." She stood then to move close to me. She parted my knees and stepped between them, her hands playing over my chest and throat.

"Poor *petit*. So alone. So lost."

I grabbed her wrist. She stiffened. I tightened my grip.

"Where will we go?" I said.

"New York. We can live by night without notice there. Anonymous and faceless with *beaucoup* places to sleep through the day undisturbed."

I pictured sleeping in filthy tunnels and cellars, feeding off the disenfranchised or unlucky. A sea of blood waiting to be lapped up from a million throats.

"Come back tomorrow night. We leave then. After dark."

I released her wrist. She took a step back, trailing her nails along my leg as she moved.

"I'll be here."

"It will be good. You will see. You will learn and I will teach you."

She walked me to the door and touched my arm. Her ebon eyes looked into mine. Her lips curled in a smile that showed a hint of white teeth.

That's when I knew for sure.

They were going to kill me.

· 25 ·

"I can't give you the same room," the weedy clerk at the Tartan said.

"They're all the same, right?" I said.

He shrugged and scooped my bills out of the slot. He passed me back a room key. A-6. Ground floor.

"And no housekeeping," I said.

"Sure. Sure." He went back to his TV.

In my new room, same as the other room except for a painting of a field of daisies instead of a herd of running horses, I went through the same light proofing ritual. Box spring against the window. Towels around the gaps of the window and door. Dresser against the door.

Nothing new on the news. No more mention of the missing corpse or the murder at the coroner's.

The sports guy was on talking about a golf tournament someplace warm.

I thought about my next move. When darkness fell I'd have to leave. I ran through my options, places I knew. Or maybe it would be better to go somewhere I'd never been. The uncertainties worried me. I needed to feed. I needed to hide. Improvisation was dangerous. There was no winging it in this life.

Only the certainty was worse. The absolute certainty that Roxanne and her cop were going to kill me if I showed up to join their road trip. I had to be just one in a long string of companions for Roxanne. Probably a hundred years or more of jilted partners behind her. My time was up. Three was a crowd. And having me free range was not in her plans. Like a black widow, she mated and she killed. When the sun went down I'd drive west.

I woke up blind.

Light was everywhere. I threw my arms over my face and rolled to the floor. The covers tangled around me.

Hands were on me. Rough hands pulled me upright. The door was wide open. The dresser lay sideways. Afternoon glare smashed at me like a physical thing.

I fought to keep them from dragging me to the door. I was weak, sick. The men were big, their grip on my arms unbreakable. I felt a searing heat on my face and hands.

"Jesus! Shut the door!"

One of the men released me and went into the source of light. I raised a hand to the one still holding me. He lifted me from my feet to slam me into the wall. The field of daisies came off its hook.

The other guy shut the door leaving only a sliver of radiance at the foot of the door.

"Sick motherfucker." The guy holding me drove a knee into my gut. I threw up a pinkish spew onto the bed. His fist in my hair, the guy slammed my face into the wall. I dropped to the floor, the world unmoored under me. The carpet heaved like an ocean storm.

"This the guy for sure?" the other one at the door said.

"Matches the photo. Thinner. Dirtier. But it's him," the guy over me said.

He had me facedown, knee in my back. He zipped plastic cuffs on my wrists. A second band went around my ankles. A new grip in my hair and he yanked me upright.

They were cops. Black uniforms, boots, gun belts. Nylon jackets with county sheriff stars on the shoulders. The other cop dumped my carry-all out onto the bed. Then my coat pockets. He came up with the carpet knife. The opening was ringed with gummy red residue.

"Well, well," he said. He flipped open a plastic bag from his pocket and dropped the knife in.

"You going to arrest me?" I said.

"You want us to arrest you?" the cop who cuffed me said.

"Just don't take me outside. I'll tell you what you want."

"Yeah. You have a condition. We heard," the other cop said. He stuffed the evidence bag in his jacket pocket.

"We're not the one you want to talk to," the cop standing over me said.

The other cop flipped on the TV and tabbed through channels to ESPN. He took a seat in the only chair. His partner sat on the edge of the bed, careful to avoid the crimson spray of vomit drying there. They became absorbed in a discussion of football draft picks. I sat between the bed and the wall, forgotten by both of them.

They were waiting.

The slit under the door turned pink, then gray and then lit by the cold radiance of the lights in the parking lot. The cops had ordered a pizza and ate it while watching a tennis tournament in shared silence. I was mostly in and out over the last of the afternoon hours, the weight of sleep heavy on me. Now I was recovering from effects of the dose of sunshine. And I was beginning to feel the need to feed. I tested the strength of the plastic bands around my wrists and ankles.

A rap at the door. One of the cops called out a "Yo!"

Chad, the redheaded cop, came into the room, eyes fixed on me.

• 26 •

They didn't take me without a fight. Even cuffed hand and foot I managed to shake off the first two cops. Chad was another story. He had my animal strength combined with a weightlifter's build. He wound up on top of me with his pistol in his hand. He brought the steel butt down on my face again and again.

I didn't lose consciousness. I'm not sure I can. The blows stunned me though. Enough to let them haul me out of the room and stuff me in the trunk of Chad's cruiser. The redhead gave me a half dozen farewell rabbit punches before slamming the door shut on me.

Jammed into a fetal position in the pitch dark, I could hear Chad speaking to the other two.

"This is the guy, right?"

"It's the guy."

"The license plate matched. But he looks different from the picture."

"It's him. He's a junkie. The dope changes them. Thanks for doing this."

"Not sure I like this being off the books."

"Live with it. You owe me, remember?"

"How many years, Chad? You're never going to forget that?"

"It's forgotten now. We're even."

They mumbled goodbyes. The door squeaked and slammed. The engine gunned and I was thrown against the spare tire.

The license plate. The kid's Hyundai. They found the body and put two and two together and it led to a car parked at the Tartan.

Now Chad had me and was taking me someplace I was sure I wouldn't like.

The road hissed and swished by beneath me. I could feel myself recovering from the dose of ultraviolet light. But I was hungry. Damn, I was hungry.

The car rolled on a while, the brake lights turning my world crimson at the stops. A tight right turn and the car came to a dead halt, engine idling. A door opened and shut. A slight shift in balance as someone took a seat by the driver. I could hear two voices in conversation, the tone not the words. Chad and a female voice.

He'd stopped to pick up Roxanne. This ride was going to end the same way it did for those kids they dropped off the bridge.

I tested the straps around my hands and feet again, applying steady outward pressure. I could feel the plastic stretching, straining. With a furious burst of sheer anger-driven strength I felt the cuff behind me snap.

It was a tight fit but I reached down to tug at the cuff around my ankle. It was an awkward angle with no room to really pull with any kind of force. I undid the laces of my sneakers and slid them off along with my socks. I stretched the cuffs enough that I could slide them down over my ankles and then my feet.

I was free.

The tires under me crunched over a broken surface a long while before coming to a full stop. My fingers found the cold surface of a tire bar. I gripped it and braced my bare feet against the inside of the rear quarter panel.

When the trunk opened I leapt and swung. Chad jumped back, eyes wide and teeth bared. I tumbled out onto sharp edged gravel. He came for me, a steel-capped boot sailing for my head. It struck a glancing blow off my shoulder as I rolled under the cop car and across a puddle of icy slush to the other side. Chad raced around the car to meet me as I regained my feet. He pulled his pistol and trained it on my head.

"*Non!* No noise!" Roxanne's voice behind me.

I whirled in time to catch her fist full in my face. I stumbled back. Chad kicked the back of a knee and the leg went out from under me. He stomped on me a while until Roxanne called him off. I was dazed and slumped against a wheel.

Roxanne crouched to grip me under the chin, her nails digging into the flesh of my neck while Chad cuffed my wrists. This time with steel handcuffs. She tilted her head to study my face.

"You are so much trouble, *mon petit*," she said.

"I thought you liked that about me," I said. Chad jerked me upright by the steel chain between my hands.

"This was never about what I like or do not like," she said. "I told you that it is all about anonymity, invisibility. Your face was on the television. In the newspapers. Too many unanswerable questions."

Chad shoved me forward across the gravel lot. There were cargo containers stacked six high in neat rows to either side. We walked to the end of the row and turned to walk along a pier. The cop held me upright as we moved down concrete steps toward the edge of a canal. The water was still and black between sheets of ice white as lace in the moonlight.

I was shoved to my knees.

"I guess this is *au revoir*," I said.

"*Non*," Roxanne said. "This is goodbye."

• 27 •

"Where is the ax?" Roxanne said.

"In the car I guess," Chad said.

"Then get it!" Roxanne said. She spat the words.

Behind me I heard the scrape of boots on the gravel scree. Roxanne's hand pressed down my shoulder. The sharp stones bit into my knees and shins.

"You're going to chop me up? That's how it's done?" I said.

"One of the ways. We will take your head first. I see no need to be cruel," she said. There was a smile in her voice. This amused her.

"And will I die? I mean, is that the end of it?"

"Eventually. There will be no pain."

"And how can you know that?"

"It is what I have been told."

I had no time to think about that. The flat crack from three explosions went off. The sound echoed to us from the steel canyon of the stacked containers. Shots from a gun followed by a voice shouting.

Roxanne's hand leapt from my shoulder. I craned my neck to see her move quietly to the head of the concrete steps. She stopped there to watch for a few seconds before running back down the steps and past me. She continued on down the tow path by the canal, cowboy boots flying.

Something she saw scared the shit out of her. That was enough for me. I struggled to get to my feet and fell on my side. Footfalls were coming from between the containers. There was a high keening scream coming from somewhere. Bouncing beams of iridescent blue light stabbed out of the dark.

My options were shrinking fast. There was one thing and one thing only that I understood about what was happening. I did not want to be here when those beams of light fell on this pier.

I dug into the gravel with a knee to set myself rolling. I rolled over to the edge of the canal and tipped myself over the side.

My body struck the ice sheet that had formed along the stone wall. The ice squeaked and popped under me as I continued to roll. I slid off the edge of the ice shelf and into the black water. I let myself sink into the cold dark. Those blue light beams played through the veneer of ice, dancing back and forth and then were gone.

I sank deeper and deeper until the soles of my bare feet touched the muck at the bottom of the canal. I panicked for a few seconds, my body thrashing, my wrists pulling on the cuffs. This lasted until I realized that my body was not reacting to any of this. No feeling of strangulation, no intense desire to breathe. I *didn't* breathe any more.

I couldn't drown.

My eyes adjusted until I could clearly see the channel of the water way. The high smooth walls rising either side, the floor littered with debris of all kinds. A car flipped on its roof. Shopping carts and an old refrigerator. I was *aware* of the cold but it caused me no pain or discomfort. With my wrists behind me I couldn't really swim. But I could walk.

I'm not sure how far I walked along the floor of the canal. Eventually I came to a place where there was an indent in the canal wall with a sloping pad rising up to the surface at a twenty degree grade. A boat slip. I walked up it to find myself on the tow path again with woods along either bank.

I followed the tow path back the way I came. The woods ended and the towers of cargo containers came into view. Moving low and staying to cover I reached a row of trucks. I made my way behind them to a place where I could see Chad's cop car where he'd parked it. The trunk was open and the driver side rear door. Nothing moved.

I dropped to hands and knees and then my belly. I crept along the side of a container until I could peek out to see behind the cop car. No one was here. The container lot was dark and quiet.

No, not entirely quiet.

From somewhere the other side of the cop car I could hear a kind of trilling sound. Like a cat or a kitten but not entirely. A cross between a mew and a wheeze.

I moved low, knees bent and fingers on the ground until I reached the cop car. I hoped the car keys were in the ignition. I was vulnerable. I had to get out of the cuffs. Crouched low, I opened the car door and felt along the steering column. No keys.

The mewling sound grew louder, more urgent. I went around the rear of the car to find Chad lying on gravel.

Well, the *sum* of him anyway.

A fire ax lay where it had been thrown. The broad blade slick with blood. Chad's arms and legs lay scattered around it where they'd been chopped from his torso. His head and torso lay separated in a puddle of red slush.

Following the whimpering sound I stood and walked to the head. Chad's eyes fixed on me, his mouth worked to form words. All that came out was the sound I'd mistaken for a cat. His eyes were pleading, his mouth a red maw with tongue moving and teeth clacking.

I ignored him and crouched by the torso, awkwardly feeling along his pants until I heard the jangle of his key ring. I managed to fish that out and, after a few tries, had the key in the cuffs and unsnapped them. I took his wallet and his hand gun. He let out a wet clucking sound as I went for the car. I turned to see him looking at me, eyes like a sad puppy.

With a swipe of my bare foot I sent Chad's head bouncing over the gravel to strike the side of a container. It struck with a satisfying bang.

I got my socks and sneakers out of the trunk and slammed it shut. I started up the car and backed it around in a half circle to gun it between the containers and out onto a surface road that curved left into some woods. The nimbus glow of the city reflected on the ceiling of low hanging clouds.

I needed to feed and I needed to hide. In that order.

· 28 ·

I rented a car with a credit card and driver's license I took off a guy I caught coming out of a strip club. Roger Thomas Downes.

He looked enough like me for me to pass. I'd be out of the state by the time they found him in the dumpster where I left him. There's a possibility I left him alive. I only fed enough to take the edge off. I told myself he'd wake up in a few hours.

Before leaving town I called in a 911 call on a sixty-unit apartment building. I told the dispatcher my father was having a heart attack. I parked outside the building and waited. An ambulance showed up, a pair of EMTs rushing into the building leaving their ride behind, lights swirling. Inside I found the cooler stuffed with blood packs and plasma. I took the cooler and was in my rental and pulling past the local fire company's rescue truck as it turned into the lot.

I had food for the road. The trip would take a few days. I could only drive at night going city to city. I had to find places where I could park long term without being towed or ticketed. They might be looking for my car. Long-term parking at airports or hotels that didn't have valet parking. I'd pull into a spot before dawn, lock up, and climb into the trunk to wait out the daylight hours.

Three nights of driving and I was in Newark. I left the rental on a street where it would be either stripped or vanish within a few hours. Took the PATH train into the city.

The only time I'd ever been to New York was on a school field trip to see *Lion King*. Two days and one night in the city my senior year of high school. All I saw then was mid-town Manhattan.

I was disappointed that all the porno places had shut down years before. I don't remember much about the show. Heather Mongelluzzo let me feel one of her tits on the long bus ride back home.

Roxanne lied to me when she told me she and her cop were heading for New York. I knew it was a story just for me. But her reasoning was good. The city was the right environment for me. Nine million souls to hide amongst. Total anonymity. It was a place so big that no one cared who you were or where you came from or why you were there. No one gave me a second glance on the street. Even if they did they'd forgotten me by the next corner.

There was a whole underground world that never saw the light of day. By train or by foot I could go almost anywhere without ever coming up onto the street. There were tunnels for the trains and utilities. Miles and miles of them.

I had enough blood packs to last me a night or two to allow me to settle in without hunting. By then I'd have a plan mapped out. I was on my own with no mentor, no guide. Manhattan was the most forgiving place I could be. I could disappear there. Buy time until I figured my way forward.

There were plenty of disenfranchised there, too. All hours of the night there were people on the streets. Lots of them were homeless or vagrant. They slept in doorways. Lay dead drunk or high on the sidewalk. When they went missing they were another statistic. Foul play wasn't even the first supposition. People would be there one day and the next day ... gone.

I read somewhere about people who used the towers coming down on 9-11 as a chance to start over. They saw that day as an exit strategy. They were gone, off to new lives and new names, leaving everyone to assume they died that day with all the others. Who could say they didn't? And the city went on. Their places were taken by others. And soon they were nothing but a picture on a wall. Barely a memory.

This city swallowed people whole.

From Battery Park to Yonkers it was all an open buffet. And if I wanted to spread out there was Jersey and four more boroughs.

The smartest choice I could have made was making New York my new hometown. That's what I thought.

Until I found out I wasn't alone.

• 29 •

I got a metro card at Grand Central and caught a subway. At 59th Street I got off and walked to the south end of the platform where I ducked under the chain. A concrete ledge with a rusting guard rail led away into a dark interrupted at intervals by the muted glow from bare bulbs inside steel cages. The lights stretched away in an endless string to infinity.

It was early enough in the evening to spend some time finding a place to hole up. Once I had a hide I could go hunting. Now that I was down in the belly of the largest mass transit train line on the planet I was free to roam over all five boroughs for the cost of one ride and never see the sun or stars. Or is London's Tube bigger? Like I care.

I didn't know that I wasn't the only one hunting.

A dimly lit alcove widened off the narrow walkway. The tile on the walls was ancient and cracked. A door with steel lattice was set into the wall. It had metal signs bolted to it that were unreadable under a decades-thick patina of greasy black residue. I tried the pull and the door swung open, the hinges groaning.

The corridor inside was barely shoulder width. It ended in a T intersection. I turned right and the corridor stopped at another latticed steel door. This time I could read the metal signs though they were fuzzy with rust around the edges. The sign told me that this warren of tunnels was all a part of the Consolidated Edison Steam Conservation Project. I noticed for the first time that the tile walls were damp. There was a puddle of water before the door. I pulled it open and stepped inside.

I had a vague memory of seeing something about this system

on one of those "how do they do that?" shows. There were steam plants all over the city and they generated live steam that was used to heat homes and businesses all over Manhattan.

The tunnel was wider here but not by much. The walls and ceiling were tile. Pipes mounted to the ceiling ran the length of the tunnel. Thick pipes with fat connectors every twenty feet. The floor was metal grates. The condensation ran off the pipes and into a gutter under the grates. I stepped along into the dark and found that there were niches set into the walls. No idea what they were there for. But they were wide enough and deep enough for me to lie supine on.

I couldn't really feel the heat. I'm not sensitive to changes in temperature these days. I could tell from the continual drip, drip, drip from the pipes that it was sweltering in here. All that meant to me was that it would be too hot for any homeless to coop in here. And I figured it was a pretty sturdy system. It was damn sure old enough. Not much chance of any maintenance men stumbling across me. This would be my starter home.

Welcome to New York.

They jumped me when I was back out in the main subway tunnel.

I was stepping out through the last lattice door. Something shoved me against a wall. Something else smashed me over the head with a bottle. A million shards of glass exploded like a galaxy around me. The combination of sheer force and surprise drove me to my knees where a pair of sneakered feet started kicking and pummeling me.

One of the feet swung for my head and I snaked out a hand to catch the ankle of the wearer. I flipped him onto his back as I stood up. The second tough guy took a step back with a hand under his coat. The hand came out with what looked like a bayonet.

The world filled with thunder then as a northbound train with six cars came rumbling past, brakes squealing as it slowed for the stop at 59th. In the lights flashing from inside the cars I could see the pair of attackers. Not kids. A pair of older guys with mean eyes and bad teeth. Or maybe old for their age due to drugs or whatever. Could have been brothers.

I caught the arm of the guy with the blade. The other one was rising from where I'd dumped him, seething between clenched teeth. I snapped the elbow of the guy with the blade. It gave way with a wet pop. His scream was lost in the rumble of the subway passing. I planted an open-hand shove into the center of his chest and he flipped over the guard rail that lined the walkway. His brother moved to shoulder check me against the wall again.

I sidestepped and caught him around the neck as he breezed past me. A poke and swipe and his throat was open. The carpet knife moved in an arc sending out a spatter that turned the light through the windows of the rushing cars a momentary crimson.

He clapped a hand to his neck, blood jetting between his fingers. He hunched away from me. I followed him down steps to the floor of gravel ballast alongside the tracks and kicked him prone. I straddled his back to pull his head up by the hair. I fed on him until long after he stopped moving. His vessels went flat and there was no more of him left. I dropped his head to the stones.

The train had passed. It was silent again. I stood up, a little groggy with a bloated feeling. That was a big guy. Like an extra helping of the good stuff. I turned to where I guessed the other man had fallen. He lay still in a heap by the tracks except for the rise and fall of his chest from breathing. His breath was raspy. Something was broken inside.

Next to him stood a little girl, maybe six or seven. I said I'm no good at kids' ages.

She had an outrageous bushy mane of kinky hair and wore what looked like a soiled communion dress. She looked at me with dark almond eyes.

"Go away, kid," I said.

The little girl turned from me to look down at the broken man lying at her feet. She brought her eyes back to me.

"Can I share?" she said.

She blinked and I saw that her eyes weren't just dark. They were black from rim to rim.

· 30 ·

Her name was Lissa.

No last name. If she ever had one.

She was turned in Mobile, Alabama by a man named Crawford. She was a half-black orphan living off the streets after her mother died of croup. A "high yella" is what she said they called her in that other time. This was before Mobile had electric lights. She thinks she was nine years old.

She's nine years old forever now.

Crawford turned her because she was young. He used her as a lure, bait. Lissa would bring victims to him.

A runaway dog or maybe she couldn't find her mother or she was lost. Sympathetic marks would respond to her story and offer to help a helpless little girl. Some would follow her for other reasons. She had no pity for them. As the years went by she had no pity for any of them.

The man, Crawford, treated her like a pet; something he owned. She lived on the dregs he left behind. He beat her. He once locked her out of the barn where they were cooping when she talked back to him. He let the sun burn her to an ashen gray before letting her in.

They moved around a lot, mostly jumping trains. Travelling by day and feeding by night. She couldn't remember how long that went on. It stopped when she locked him in a steel-walled box car and took off on her own. Lissa never saw him again and never knew what happened to him. She liked to think that he was eventually dragged out of the car by railroad bulls. She could picture him lying on the ties screaming as the noonday sun fried him to a crisp.

"How long ago was that?" I said. We lay on shelves across from one another inside a steam tunnel.

"Can't recall. The nights don't measure like days, you know what I mean?" she said.

She was right. Without the passage of the sun in the sky the movement of time was harder to measure, to feel. This life was one long endless night measured only by the shape of the moon.

"The movies didn't have sound yet," she said after a while.

"You like movies?"

"They're fine. No one takes notice of a kid alone in a movie theater at night. They reckon the kid is with his parents. Lots of dark places to coop in a theater."

"Makes sense."

"I like libraries better. Even more places to hide and all those books to read."

"There's a big library here in the city, right?"

"Used to be I spent a lot of nights there. Then they put motion sensors in."

"You can trip those? *We* can trip those?"

"Can't fool them like cameras."

"Good to know," I said.

"I'll show you the city when the night comes. Show you things you never seen. Teach you things you never knew," she said. Her voice was solemn in the pitch dark.

As the dreamless sleep pulled me under I wondered if I was up to the responsibility of looking after a kid.

Yeah, I had *that* all wrong.

Lissa was a child in form but not in mind. She would never

grow up in the physical sense. She'd lived three or four lifetimes of experiences. A near century on her own in the city gave her a wisdom that was as deep as her unshakeable calm. And a profound cynicism that came from seeing the world from the gutter and viewing every soul you met as your next meal.

"I meet other kids like me sometimes. They're feral things. Trapped in the mind of a child, unable to reckon with the things they see and do."

"Why are you different?" I said.

"Just because. Folks always said I had an old soul."

In this new relationship I was the child and she was the endlessly patient adult guiding me through this new world.

"This French woman was a damned fool," she said. Her little girl voice was sharp with scorn.

"I didn't have a lot of choice in mentors," I said.

We sat together on a bench in Central Park and watched the moon shimmer on the pond under a cold, cloudless sky. It was early evening and couples moved by huddled together under the amber lights. Joggers trotted past in singles, pairs and larger groups. We were just a dad and his little girl enjoying a chilly evening on the town. We held hands, her fingers tiny in mine.

"Leaving a trail of dead folks everywhere she went. That's no way to avoid trouble. Draws interest to you. You don't want attention of any kind," she said.

I told her about the car accident. The day spent in the cold locker. The men who found us and left Chad without a head.

"You ever have trouble like that? People hunting you?"

"Those weren't people. Not *live* ones anyways."

"Wait. What? You mean they were like us?"

She sighed.

"How do you think something like this stays a secret so long?

Just like anywhere else there's a boss. There's someone looking out to mind things. To keep the world the way they like it."

"A boss? You mean a guy in a cape living in a castle somewhere?"

"That's all bullshit." She used the word with an authority that came from experience.

"But there's one guy? On top? A world order?"

"His name is Vikram. And he's old. So old nobody knows how old. And he's the minder of folks like us. He keeps tabs. Keeps an eye out. His folks are everywhere. And the last thing Vikram likes is rogues making a mess of things. Taking more than they need and leaving bodies behind."

"Vikram? What kind of name is that? Is it a first name?"

"It's his *name*. That's all you need. We all know who Vikram is. And he likes to keep the world in the dark about his doings and he hates it when a rogue steps out of line. The world the way it is, stories travel faster than they ever did before. Everybody knows the same thing at the same time almost. Used to be once a few bloodless bodies turn up in China nobody but a Chinaman knew about it. Now the world knows. And enough bodies turning up in Mexico, Egypt, and Ohio make people notice. Makes it a mystery. And you know what curious nuisances people can make of themselves."

"This Vikram. His people anyway. They killed Chad? And maybe Roxanne?" I said.

"Sounds like them. I seen them work once. I was part of a tribe for a while. They got sloppy. Vikram's folks showed up in the middle of the night. They don't fool. I hid till it was over."

"Are they looking for me?"

She shrugged, lips pouted.

"No ways to know. You did the right thing coming here. And you got damned lucky meeting me. I can school you. Keep you on the narrow path."

"By not leaving bodies behind?"

"Uh huh," she said.

"But I still have to feed. And some of us need more than you," I said.

"You eat all your meals in one place. I mean, back when you were living?"

"No."

"Eat all of them at once? Breakfast? Supper?"

"Unh uh."

"Same now. No need to guzzle when you can sip. It's more work sometimes but lots safer." She hopped off the bench, hands in the pockets of a wool coat two sizes too big for her. The hem slapped the back of her bare calves as she walked. I followed her around the pond toward a park exit.

"Not sure what you mean," I said.

"Take a little from this one. Little from that one till you have what you need."

"Don't people object to having a vein opened by a total stranger?"

"There's more than enough folks in a city this big never notice if you cut them. Drunks and hopheads almost anywhere you look—if you know where to look."

"Hopheads." I laughed.

"Something wrong with what I said?" She cut me a cross look.

"Just funny hearing that. Nobody calls them that anymore."

"I don't trifle myself with keeping up with modern parlance." She said it with a huff. We stood at a crosswalk watching taxis zip by.

"I noticed."

"If you're going to make fun of me . . ."

"Not at all. You're the teacher," I said.

"Damn right," she said. She squeezed my hand and stepped across the street toward a row of grand old hotels that faced the park along 59th.

• 31 •

Lissa was right.

The city was a Las Vegas buffet.

A lot of nights we didn't need to go up to the surface. There were addicts and drunks to be found on the station platforms and concourses. We'd find them lying insensate or nodding. Lissa called them lambs. She and I would playact that we knew them.

"Uncle Billy, we've been looking for you everywhere."

People walked past without even a look. We'd get the lamb up on his feet and walk him someplace more private. Lissa would open one of the smaller vessels on an arm using a folding straight razor she wore on her back suspended from a thong around her neck. We'd each take enough to bring the hunger under control. I'd apply pressure to the cut for a moment or two. After a movie or a walk in the starlight we'd move on to another lamb. The hunting got easier and the pickings fatter the later it got.

The ones we fed on would wake up with a cut they wouldn't remember getting. Maybe a hazy memory of someone helping him up. Any wooziness from blood loss would just be part of their hangover.

Lissa was expert at determining the level of blotto our victims were experiencing.

"Listen to their breathing. Watch their hands," she said. She'd give the leg an experimental kick. If they came around and could speak in complete sentences we moved on.

I was surprised at first at how many we found dead. Overdoses. It's hard to feed on the dead. No assisting internal pressure. And the blood tastes skunky like beer gone bad. There were enough pickings that we could be somewhat discerning in our tastes.

We were feeding off the bottom. Most of the alkies and druggies we found were lifers. Deadbeats made homeless by their addictions. Their clothes smelled rancid and their bodies crawled with lice and sores. Their blood had the sour aftertaste of malnourishment and whatever toxins they took in to feed their jones. None of those toxins affected us. The blood of a heroin addict didn't make us high just as the blood of a drunk didn't give us a buzz. Still, they offered a poor vintage.

"We can do better," I said.

We were walking the dark tracks under Seventh Avenue toward our recent home in an old L.I.R.R. car parked in a string on a siding.

"How so?" she said.

"A better class of lambs. Something richer than the fare we get down here in the tunnels."

"We do well enough. I'm satisfied."

"You're not satisfied. You just got used to it."

She shrugged.

"This is my life now. I don't want to spend it as some ... thing crawling in the dark like a ..." I said.

"Salamander?" she said.

"Yes. Like that."

"Salamanders are happy enough."

"Because they have to be. They don't know better. We do. We lived different lives before this. You remember?"

"I don't have much *to* remember. Nothing *good* anyways. I've been as I am now mostly all my time in this world."

I hadn't thought of that. Lissa was as I knew her for a lot longer than she was ever a little girl. I'd spent only a few months in my current state. Most of my memories were of that other life.

"I might be a monster but I don't want to live like one," I said.

"We're not monsters. We're part of life. As much a part of life as a tiger or a flea. There's a purpose to us being this way. Has to be," she said.

"We're in God's plan?"

"Some kind of plan, else why would we be like this?"

We reached the row of cars on the dark siding. Inside they smelled of caked grease and old rust. I beat on a seat cushion, causing a nest of mice to flee before lying back on it. Lissa climbed up to an overhead luggage rack where she had a blanket spread.

"Tomorrow night we spread our wings a little," I said. I rested my head on a stack of moldering newspapers.

She answered with a dry laugh.

"Now we're *flying* salamanders," she said.

"That's right. Rising out of the mud to take Manhattan."

She was quiet now, not even the sound of breathing from atop the blanket above me. All I could see of her were her sneakers, pink with little blue flowers. She was old enough to be my grandmother's mother. In her quiet times it was hard to think of her that way. Her face was the face of an angel when she slept. There was no trace of the thing she had become.

Maybe she was right. Maybe we were part of God's plan somehow. We had a place in the grand scheme of things.

And, starting the next night, that place was going to be south of 14th.

• 32 •

We topped off with a tweaker we found lying on a bench in Madison Park. He was crashed after days of smoking crank. The stink of it was on him. The sharp chemical taste of it was in his blood. We only took enough to quench the thirst for a bit and left him in the bushes at the base of a tree.

It was my idea to hit the after-hours clubs that were dotted all over Tribeca, NoHo, SoHo and the Village. Some legal and some not. The clubs came and went. Popping up overnight to burn bright and loud, and disappearing as the tides of trendiness swept in and out to take some places away and replace them with others like shiny pebbles on a beach.

There were pay-to-enter parties in lofts and raves in cellars. Many never advertised and you either heard of them by word of mouth or you followed the boom of the music to the latest place to be. Or looked for a line of limos and taxis waiting at the curb.

What *was* constant was a clientele on the younger side with a self-destructive attraction to liquor and drugs. A better class of junkie. A drunk in designer clothes. They smelled better and the blood tasted sweeter. They also had cash and jewelry on them they wouldn't miss. And if they missed them they'd consider the loss the price of having a hell of a night. Even if it was a night they couldn't remember. The one thing they'd never notice was the tiny cut on their wrist or ankle surrounded by a purple circle of bruising.

Lissa would wait nearby in a doorway or alley, anywhere that let her keep an eye on any exits. Dressed in a designer suit jacket I lifted from a blotto Wall Street drunk a few nights before, I'd troll the bar. I was looking for anyone stupefied enough to be pliable but not so fried they couldn't walk out with me.

The first night I sidled up to a guy propped on his elbows at a marble-topped bar. His head was dipping and rising out of time with the music thrumming from speakers in the ceiling. He had an armada of empties in front of him and the change from a hundred lying in a pool of spilled vodka.

"Slow here tonight," I shouted. I bumped his shoulder with mine.

He turned his head in slow motion. Eyes red and unfocused. Mouth slack. An expensive suit and even more expensive watch. He smelled of vomit. This was a serious bender.

"You said?" he said.

"Slow! Slow in here tonight! No talent!"

"Talent?"

"Pussy!" I shrieked in his ear.

He turned, distracted by the barman scooping a twenty from his change and dropping a few bills and change in its place by a fresh V&T on ice.

"Used to be better here. But all the hot honeys are going to that place on Perry."

He turned back to me.

"What place?"

"Roxanne's," I said. The first name I thought of.

"Sounds sexy." It came out, "zouns zessy."

"Bet your ass. Models. Art school students. All kinds of pussy." Full pimp mode me.

"I know you?" His twisted features loomed closer.

"Yeah. Bill Nordling. That conference in . . . in . . ."

"Vegas. You were with Goldman." He poked an unsteady finger into my chest.

"Used to be. Moved down the street. You know how it is."

He nodded sagely, no more idea of what I was talking about than I did. He swept all but a ten and the loose change from the bar and stuffed the other bills in his coat pocket.

"You're right, Bill. This place sucks. No ass." It came out, "you rye, Bill. Zis place suss."

I took his arm to help him slide off the stool. Together we weaved along the edge of the dance floor toward a fire exit. The fug of hot sweat coming off the pack of dancers stoked the fire in my belly.

He started to revive in the cold gust of air that struck us as we stepped into the alley. I felt his arm tighten on mine. There was some serious gym muscle under the Armani sleeve.

"Shit. We need to get a cab," he said. His voice was less slurred now.

"Daddy? Mama sent me to bring you home."

We both turned as one to Lissa stepping from the shadows deeper in the alley. She wore a woeful expression, hands clutched together. I'm not sure if it was knowledge of her true nature but she looked like she walked out of an old tintype. Her voice quavered, her dark eyes wet. But not with tears.

"This your little girl?" the drunk said. He straightened. His arm started to pull from mine.

"That's my daddy," she said before I could speak.

"We can walk her home then catch a cab. My place is just down this way," I said. I renewed my grip on his arm to steer him farther into the alley, into the shadows cast by the bars of fire escapes above.

He fought to pull away from me. I tightened up, yanking him closer to me.

"You tell me where this place is. Meet me there," he said. He grunted with the effort to free himself.

"You'll never find it without me."

"Then forget it. I think I had enough."

He made one final effort to take his arm back. I turned, swinging him against my hip. His feet left the ground and I flung him against a dumpster where he hit his head on the steel lip. He dropped to the slick paving, deflated. He didn't move.

Lissa glided past me to drop to her knees by him. The razor came out of her coat and she flicked it open. She made a tiny slit where the heel of his hand met his wrist. I slipped the Breitling from his other wrist before plucking a wallet from his inside coat pocket and a money clip from his pants.

I took my turn at his wrist when Lissa was done. The pulse was slow and weak. It took effort to draw the blood out. I wondered if he was dying. We left him there, propped against the dumpster. We went down to the station at Lafayette and caught an express uptown.

· 33 ·

"Everything worth doing starts out badly. There's a learning curve," I said.

"You read that someplace?" Lissa said.

She was walking the tracks ahead of me. Somehow those little legs moved fast enough that I had to jog to keep up. I tripped on a chipped concrete tie and went stumbling. I ran to get to her side again.

"It was better than feeding off junkies and winos. And we have some money. That watch is worth five thousand minimum."

"Money? What's the good of money? You going to hire a lawyer with it when you get caught?"

"Come on, Lissa. The police aren't going to catch us."

She turned to me. A local slowly trundling by made sparks that lit Lissa's face a ghostly white. Her eyes turned to swirling black smoke, fixed on mine until the sound of the passing cars faded away.

"Ain't about police. I told you. Ain't about getting arrested and, if you're lucky, when the sun comes up, you cook down to gristle and bones in a cell somewheres."

"Vikram. This mystery guy. Some kind of original gangsta."

"No mystery. No mystery. You left a witness behind. That man wasn't no ways drunk enough to forget you. Or forget me."

"He might be dead. His pulse was weak," I said. I regretted it.

Her brows knitted over those eyes, those ancient, damning eyes.

"Don't follow me," she said. She stormed away down the tracks, her skinny legs flashing under the swaying hem of the coat.

Feeling sorry for myself, I paused long enough to lose her. When I chased down the way she went I couldn't find her. I searched until just before day broke on the streets above, walking tracks and platforms from under Penn Station to Grand Central. She wasn't cooping in any of our usual places.

Walking along the tracks, avoiding shafts of gray light coming down through sidewalks vents above, I found a ladder by the tracks just south of the 51st Street metro platform. I climbed along a steel joist to wedge myself back into a brick-walled recess. I could hear the street traffic overhead and the rolling thunder of the trains below as the sleep claimed me.

I was still hungry and my belly and limbs burned with need. Sharper than that was another sensation almost as painful.

I felt alone.

• 34 •

The commodities broker, that's what he was, from the night before made the papers. He didn't die but was comatose in an ICU at Presbyterian. Page seven in the *News*. Page eleven in the *Post*. I didn't see the *Times*. No one left a copy on any of the cars on the subway car I was taking to Bushwick.

From the window I watched the black surface of the river rush by below the tracks. The lights of the cars reflected on the water. The train was running suspended under the Williamsburg Bridge. After the fuck-up of the night before I thought it was a good idea to leave the city for Brooklyn. There were clubs there. Plenty of bars. The place was gentrifying, moving on up. Lots of fresh thoroughbred blood on the hoof.

I had a couple of thousand dollars on me from the billfold and from maxing out the broker's debit cards at ATMs all over Midtown. No one thought to close his accounts after the mugging. Couldn't believe the chump had his pin number written down on a slip of paper inside his wallet. And good luck to anyone checking the video off the ATM. I held onto the watch. Chances were there was a bulletin out to pawn shops. I'd have to find another way to move it.

Or keep it. The watch was flashy enough to match the rest of my cheesy ensemble. It was part of my protective camouflage of a club crawler. I spent some of the cash on a new jacket and some shirts. A nice pair of alligator loafers. All black to fit in with the look of all the other people riding the subway. Everyone in the city looks like they're dressed for a funeral all the time. Especially in the cold months. Coats, caps, scarves all in black. The only flashes of color were the occasional ribbon showing off the wearer's pet cause.

I didn't need Lissa for this, I decided. A kid was a distraction in the world I was prowling. I was better off as a lone wolf. It gave me more options, room to improvise.

It took a fifty to get past the bouncer at the first club. He didn't like the look of a lone wolf. Gave me a warning glare from his pig eyes as he parted the rope for me. I grinned back and winked over the top of a shiny new pair of Oakleys.

Inside the place was loud enough to blister the paint off the walls. Everything was rimmed in long strands of blue and orange neon. The crowd was mostly white in a neighborhood that was mostly brown only a few years back. I heard conversations in a mix of languages as I threaded the crowd for a section of a long curving bar that ran the length of the building beyond the dance floor. The booths were no good for me and most of them were full to bursting anyway.

I ordered a club soda that I pretended to drink and watched the crowd crushed against the bar. I was starving. The smell of sweat and the rhythm of all those heartbeats was driving me crazy. It was early though. Too early for anyone to be in the condition I needed them to be in. So I watched the room; the young bodies moving under the pulsing lights in time to an incessant beat crashing from speakers mounted high in the black-painted ceiling of what was once a department store from the look of it.

Most customers only stayed at the bar long enough to get one of a half dozen busy bartenders' attention, grab their drinks, and head back to their booth. A few stayed at the bar, sipping drinks and noshing on the world's most expensive bowls of mixed nuts and pretzels.

A guy and girl sitting just around the next curve caught my eye. The guy was practically a mirror image of me; the perfect picture of the look I was going for but probably pulling it off better than me. Black on black suit, blond hair that looked like it was permed, and a tattoo of a two-headed eagle spreading its wings above the collar line. Gold chains, a diamond stud in one lobe. The girl was a pneumatic blonde in what looked like a rubber dress that stopped way up on her thighs. The lights turned her hair from silver to white to iridescent blue from second to passing second.

These two were there to be seen. I wondered if they arrived together or met by chance. Their heads were close together in shouted conversation. He had his hand on her leg and she didn't mind. She twiddled his tie in her fingers, at one point clenching the end of it between her teeth.

It struck me that one or the other of them might be in the same game I was. I watched closely to see that they were drinking their drinks. He had a couple of long necks, imports with labels I didn't recognize. She had a tall slim tumbler with something green over crushed ice. I watched her drain it, sucking the last of it through the straw. The guy gestured and a bartender glided up. I almost missed it. A look passed between them, a silent acknowledgement. The guy laid a hundred on the bar and the bartender slid it out of sight to come back with a fresh drink for the lady.

And no change.

A very special drink. A very expensive drink.

I kept watching as the girl downed half of the new drink. A few pulls on the straw and she began to lose her poise. The level in the glass fell and she began to lose her balance. The guy slipped a hand around her waist, holding her up. He had his lips close to her ear. He said something that made her nod slowly, her mouth slack now. A faraway look in her eyes.

They brushed past me on the way to a lounge area off the main room. I followed as they passed rows of booths packed with people hollering at each other in what passed for conversation. The guy in black and the girl in rubber stumbled/walked down a hall lined either side with the openings to men's and women's lounges. The guy was almost carrying her at this point, the toes of her high-heels making furrows in the carpet. He was taking her past the rest rooms for a fire door at the end of the hallway.

I caught up, drawing alongside them. I put out an arm to block their way. The girl's head swayed on her neck and she made an effort to look at me. Blue eyes registered nothing, the pupils open wide like buttons. The guy swiped out a hand to brush me aside.

"I think I know her," I said.

"Yeah? She don't know you," he said. Trace of an accent.

I got a hand between them and pulled her out of his grip. With a push to the small of her back I launched her into the women's room entrance. She was caught up in a gaggle of other women heading in and swept along.

The guy made a grab for my throat. His face was bunched in animal rage. I caught his wrist and had him turned around with his hand driven up between his shoulders. He yelped once as I marched him into the men's. The room was empty. The smell of piss was driving me mad. I slammed him into the first stall I came to. He made to fight me, hands braced on the stall walls. I drove his head hard enough against the tiles to crack a few.

He was cold cocked but still semi-conscious when I sat him down on the commode. His eyes swam in the sockets. Blood trickled through white powder from the cracked tile. His mouth moved like he was chewing his tongue. I rifled his pockets and came up with a fat wad of cash in a rubber band, a vial of some kind of white powder, a gold cigarette case and a receipt from valet parking. Tucked into his waistband at the back was a little pistol. I know shit about guns. I guess it was an automatic. I guessed it wasn't legal either.

The guy started making moaning noises. I wadded up some toilet paper and stuffed it in his mouth. He tried to focus his eyes on me but gave up to just stare into the infinite.

I dropped to my knees in front of him and rolled up a sleeve of his jacket. I opened a small vein on the side of his wrist and dropped my head to feed.

Outside the stall I heard shoe soles scrape on the tiles to approach the wall of urinals.

"Jesus Christ. You see this?" one guy said.

"What?" the other guy said.

"You didn't tell me it's that kinda club," the one guy said.

"What are you gonna do about it?" the other guy said.

· 35 ·

An ambulance arrived. Two cops parted the crowd for a pair of EMTs with a folding gurney. The music didn't stop for a beat. A hundred phones came out to record the event.

I pretended to nurse a club soda and watched them roll the guy out of the men's room. His head was strapped into a brace. No sign of the blonde in the rubber dress. She was probably sitting catatonic in a toilet stall.

It was a risk to stay, maybe. The cops left after a few words with one of the bartenders. The bartender shrugged and shook his head. The cops left. Simple assault and robbery. Happens a hundred times a night. The beat went on.

I dumped the club soda into a faux potted plant and went for a refill. I grabbed a section of rail closest to the bartender who served special drinks at a hundred a pop. I tipped my glass at him and he took it.

"Club soda again?"

"Yeah. I'm designated driver. My brother's bachelor party." I mimed regret.

"Shoulda sprung for a limo. Or Uber."

"Hindsight."

He shouldered past another bartender and topped off my glass from a syphon.

"Does it ever slow down in here?" I nodded toward the mob packed before the DJ stage.

"Around six. We close by seven usually. I'm out of here at four."

"You must hate this job."

"Naw! The money is crazy! I dropped out of pre-med to do this." He scooped up the twenty I set on the bar.

Dropped out of pre-med. But he was still into pharmaceuticals.

The valet, a black kid in a parka worn over a tuxedo shirt, took the receipt from my hand and charged toward a lot down the block. I looked enough like the guy with the accent to pass. Or maybe he only had eyes for the fifty I stuffed into his hand. The valet was back inside of five minutes with a black BMW two-seater gleaming wet with snow melt.

I pulled down the block. No traffic at this hour. I hung a U-turn and pulled into an open slot that gave me a view of the front of the club. There was no line out front now. More partiers were coming out now than going in. Cabs pulled up now and again to let die-hards out. The night was moving toward morning, the club scene giving way to the working day.

The bartender who wanted to be a doctor came out just after four. He crossed the street and hiked toward me, head down and collar of a woolen coat pulled up. Hands in coat pockets. I rolled the window down as he passed.

"Hey. You want a ride?"

He stopped, bent to squint at me.

"Yeah? I know you?"

"Club soda."

"What happened to your brother's bachelor party?"

"That was bullshit." No reason to keep up the sham. He already knew it was a lie.

"I'm not gay." He turned to go on.

"I'm talking business," I called.

He spun and came back.

"What kind of business?"

"What do you use? Pills? Powder?"

He studied me with new eyes.

"You a cop, club soda?"

"No. I want to buy."

"Show me the cash."

I knew better than that.

"You have anything on you?" I said.

"Fifty pills. Rohypnol. Three-thirteen grams. And some I crushed in a bottle."

"How much for what you have?"

It was a thousand even. I peeled it off the rubber-banded roll. He handed over a baggie of pills and a tiny plastic bottle with a pop-off lid.

"You can get more?"

"All you want. Clonazepam. Lorazepam. Ecstasy. Viagra. I can hook you up."

"You here most nights?"

"Thursday through Sunday. You need my cell?"

"I'll find you," I said. I pulled out of the slot. I could see him in the rear view watching me before he turned away to walk on.

The pills lay on the leather seat next to me. I was still hungry but the sun would be coming up over Long Island in little more than an hour. I found a parking garage wedged between two buildings. It was a reserved lot for a condo complex two blocks over. For a hundo the attendant gave me a spot on the third floor as long as I was gone by evening. No problem, brother.

I pulled in snug between a Lincoln and an Infinity. No windows. No sunlight. I pulled the lever and dropped the seat back as far as it would go, my head below the windows behind deeply tinted glass. I lay there waiting to slide into darkness.

The evening went well. I had a whole new plan. I had this town figured out. I had it by the ass. This was going to work out for me, all on my own. No help from anyone. The sun was going to set on a brand new me when this day was over.

• 36 •

The pills went fast. Two, sometimes three a night. I moved around clubs all over Brooklyn. Gay and straight. Techno, salsa and blues.

Dosing a victim was easier than I expected. Drunks don't have much in the way of discretion. Especially men. Some of them even took a pill willingly when I offered it. When they had questions I just told them it was something new.

The roofies kicked in fast, faster if the takers were already intoxicated. They were conscious but pliable. No problem shepherding them into an alley, garage or back room to feed. If the club was dark enough and noisy enough, I'd find an empty booth and feed there. A nick of the small vein on the side of the wrist at the base of the thumb was all it took. It looked like a more innocent public display of affection than what was going on in other booths.

I was back for a new buy two weeks later.

"I'm not carrying tonight," the bartender said.

"I have cash," I said. And I did. I took more than blood off my prey. My roll was fat with large bills.

"We've had cops in here the last few nights. I'm laying low."

"But I need more."

"You out already? That was fifty pills. It's only been what? Two weeks? You some kind of sex maniac?"

"I want to build a stash. Five hundred pills to start."

He eyed me hard before getting out a pen to write on the back of a coaster. He slid it across to me.

"I'm closing tonight then I have a thing. Call me in the afternoon," he said.

"Night's better for me. I have a thing too."

"Okay. Cool. I'll set you up." He pushed away to take drink orders from a tipsy pair of girls next to me.

I moved on to grab a cab for a new club in Bed-Stuy. Virgin hunting ground.

"Yeah?" The bartender picked up on the other end.

"It's me." We weren't on a first or last name basis.

"You still interested? Five hundred?"

"That's why I'm calling."

He paused. I could hear a basketball game on the TV behind him. He gave me an address in Bushwick a few blocks from the club where he worked.

"When can you be here?"

"Thirty minutes. I'm getting a cab now."

He broke the connection.

The cab dropped me off on a street lined either side with storefronts. Older businesses like a dry cleaner and a pharmacy shared the street with newer, trendier stores. A coffee shop with a cute name, a health food store, pet clinic and a 24-hour gym.

The address the bartender gave me had a vestibule with a brass panel of buttons. I rang the one under the name Worley. After a beat or two the door buzzed in response and I pushed in.

It was a third floor walk-up and the door was ajar. Color commentary and ambient crowd noise from inside. Guy liked his basketball. I knocked my knuckles on the jamb. No entry without an invitation.

"Come on in," the bartender called from inside.

I stepped inside. The bartender muted the b-ball game and greeted me with a fixed smile. He stepped past me to close the door and snap a pair of deadbolts in place.

"That necessary?" I said.

"The neighborhood isn't one hundred percent gentrified yet." A new voice.

Three men stepped from a back room. A smaller man in corn rows and two giants with heads shaved smooth. The bartender ducked away toward a corner near the windows, his eyes wide and darting.

"Friends of yours?" I said. The bartender just stared.

"You're looking to buy a serious shitload of pills," the smallest of the trio said. He might have looked ludicrous with tiny pigtails sprouting from his head but for the face below them. A face bunched like a fist in a perpetual scowl that revealed yellow teeth capped with silver. His eyes were yellow, too, and fixed on me with a predator's glare. Scarred hands gleamed with rings. He was all thug but dressed for Wall Street in a cashmere coat worn over a designer suit and Italian loafers.

The man mountains behind him were dressed closer to their function. Sweats worn under starter jackets.

"So, I'm buying from the source. Does that mean a discount?" I said. I smiled easy. His scowl deepened.

"You gonna jew me down now?"

He stepped closer to press fingers into my chest. His eyes narrowed to slits when his shove didn't move me. He pressed harder and I allowed him to shove me back into a chair.

"You ain't using this shit on your own. You're looking to sell." He put a foot up on a coffee table, allowing me to see a shiny silver revolver tucked into a holster strapped over a sock.

"At these prices? There's no room for profit there."

"So you usin' this shit yourself? Bullshit. Even rabbits don't need that much pussy. You a rabbit?"

"Well, I'm *some* kind of animal." I smiled at him.

He recoiled at that. His yellow eyes blazed with a new heat.

"See what this motherfucker's got," he said. He stepped back and waved the giants in.

I lunged out of the chair for them, the last thing the giants expected. They were used to fear in their victims. One swipe of the carpet knife opened the throat of one of them. Blood showered over the room. The other put up a defensive hand and my blade ripped a wound across the spread fingers. The big man stepped back, swinging his arm to send a spray of blood that spattered the smaller man. I drove in closer to get the giant by the throat and carry him before me across the room. I slammed him hard against a wall and watched his lips turn blue.

The sound of the little revolver filled the room once, twice. I felt a pair of swift punches to my back. I turned to see the little man standing with the pistol aimed straight-armed at me. The bartender stood backed into a corner with eyes goggling and mouth moving in a silent plea.

I stepped to the little man as he let fly until his little gun was empty. A third round took me in the chest. The final two went wild and then I had him by the neck. I pulled him close to me, our faces inches from one another. I lifted his feet from the floor to bring us level. His panting breath in my face smelled like tobacco and mint.

And the heady musk of fear.

He jerked in time with two muffled blasts from my own pistol that I stabbed tight into his side. The mean face went slack. The light faded from the yellow eyes turning them to tarnished gold. I released him to drop to the floor.

The bartender stared first at the little dead man on the floor and then at me. He sucked in a lungful of breath that I knew would come out in a scream. I stepped over the little man and drove the end of my gun's barrel into his open mouth and pulled the trigger twice. Blood, bone and brains were fired up the walls and ceiling like they came from a hose.

I turned a chair around to face the big man seated against the wall, sucking in breath. He held his wounded hand to his chest where blood stained his sweat suit black. His eyes were on me. His mouth a wet oval with the effort to draw the next breath into his bruised windpipe.

I sat listening, the pistol warm on my knee. There were no sirens in the distance. No voices in the hallway. The bartender was right. This neighborhood had not totally surrendered to the gentry.

"Everybody's dead, friend. Everybody but you," I said.

The big man relaxed a bit when I stood up, leaving the pistol on the arm of the chair.

"So you're the only one who's any good to me." I took the carpet knife from my jacket pocket and slid the blade free.

He didn't have the breath to scream.

• 37 •

My clothes were soaked in blood. My hair was sticky with the stuff. I took a hot shower in the bartender's bathroom. My fingers explored the bullet holes in my torso. There was no pain. And no blood, of course. There would be no healing either. The flesh along the lips of the wounds was whitish. I could insert my finger into them up to the second knuckle. I remembered the wound Roxanne showed me.

My pistol was covered in blood too. I left it on the bathroom floor on top of my sodden clothes.

I toweled off and went into the bedroom to find fresh clothes. I dropped them to the floor instead. Here I was full, satisfied. Frankly, too logy from feeding to face hunting up a new coop.

I went back to the living room and stepped around the sticky pools of blood to head for the door. I shot the bolts and secured the steel bar of a police lock in place. On my way back to the bedroom I pulled the phone lines from the wall. I drew the blinds and secured blankets over the pair of windows that faced an airshaft. Naked, I lay atop the covers. There were some magazines on a nightstand. *Men's Health* and *Forbes*. I thumbed through them until sleep took me, surrendering to the comforting warmth of a good feed.

When night came again I searched the apartment. I found baggies of pills, in different shapes and colors, hidden inside a coffee pot in the kitchen. I pulled out the drawers of a dresser to find plastic-wrapped stacks of bills taped to the undersides. In the pockets of the men in the living room I found more cash, credit cards, a stiletto knife, and a set of car keys with a key remote. The little man's shiny little revolver lay by a leg of the sofa. I picked that up. In a coat pocket I found some loose shells that seemed to fit it. I took them too.

I did the search as fast as I could. The stench of dried blood was sickening. Like spoiled food mixed with feces. There was plenty of that, too. The bartender had let go of a pantload when I blasted twin holes in his skull.

In a closet I found stuff near enough to my size for an acceptable change of clothes. Cotton shirt, khakis, sneakers and a leather bomber jacket. It would do until I could buy a new suit for club hopping. I took a last look around the place before turning the locks. Blood on the walls, floor and ceiling. Bullet holes in walls. Fingerprints everywhere, including mine. I wouldn't be seeing Brooklyn for a while.

Out in the street I walked the block, pressing the tab on the key remote I found in one of the big men's pockets. I walked to one corner then back to the other. A horn hooted somewhere. Around the corner an electric blue SUV was pulled to the curb. The lights blinked and it hooted again when I pressed the tab. There were parking tickets under the wiper. I tore them free and threw them to the street.

The car was a beast and roared to life like one. Monster woofers in the rear made the whole car shiver when some minor chord hip-hop masterpiece came blasting from the speakers. I cut the music off and pulled out onto the street to start the ride back to Manhattan.

I left it parked with two wheels up on the curb of a narrow alley in East Village. A quick search turned up a cut down shotgun under one seat and a stun gun under another. I pressed the toggle on the stun gun. A humming and crackling bar of blue electricity arced between the contact points. I left the shotgun and pocketed the Taser. Leaving the SUV unlocked and the keys in the ignition, I walked south toward a club on Broome that I hadn't been to in a while. It was frequented by college kids and my borrowed clothes would fit right in.

I was hungry again.

• 38 •

There's a limit to what money can buy. Real money, cash, is almost worthless in so many places. In a world afraid of its own shadow, it's nearly impossible do anything significant without a credit card and photo ID. Unless I wanted to spend the rest of my existence sleeping on rafters or in abandoned trucks, I'd need both.

First I'd need a new identity. The hardest part of that was a driver's license or any other kind of identification that involved a photograph. A picture of a backdrop was not going to get it done. I wished that I'd kept a photo of myself from before. There was my portrait on the Handley-Barker website unless they took it down. But that unctuous smile and three-quarter view against a background of maple trees was all wrong for an official photo.

I searched through the collection of wallets I'd collected for a driver's license that had a picture of someone close enough in appearance to me that I could pass for them. That brings up another problem I was having. I had a bagful of stolen stuff. Cash, watches, jewelry and wallets. Along with that a baggie with enough soporifics to put the whole city in a trance. And the little man's revolver and extra ammunition. I couldn't keep carrying that around with me everywhere and I couldn't keep checking it in clubs along with my coat. Only a matter of time before a check girl either called the cops or took off with what amounted to two years' salary.

I'm not sure what a check girl at a club makes but it has to be in the neighborhood of forty kay with tips. That's what my ever-growing roll, or rolls, had grown to. I could live a lot more comfortably, and a lot more securely, on a wad like that for quite a while. Especially when you consider what I saved by never eating.

One of the pieces of ID I had was a passport for a guy from the Netherlands. That wouldn't matter. I only needed the photo. His face was roughly the shape of mine but his hair was darker. He had a goatee but that wasn't happening. I shaved once after the night this all started and never saw evidence of facial hair again. Still, that might even help with the disguise. He was two inches taller than me but who notices things like that? It's not like I was planning any international travel.

Cruising the clubs I met plenty of sketchy people. It wasn't hard, after a few questions, to find someone to help me become a new me. That's how I found Tariq. He was Iraqi or Iranian or what does it matter? He spoke with a North Jersey accent as thick as Travolta's.

"You need a social. That's five hundred. You need a credit card to match your ID. I can get you a legit one, no problem," he said.

"An actual credit card?" I said.

We were in his Audi, cruising down FDR, the lights of apartment towers looming along the bank above us. Row after row of high rise hives.

"Yeah. The real thing. You use it, the bills come, you pay them. When you don't want to pay them no more? Fuck it. No way they can dun someone doesn't exist, am I right?"

I nodded.

"We can go to a place I know. Take your picture. That's another hundred."

"No picture. Use this," I said. I handed over the passport. He held it open against the steering wheel.

"This you?" he said.

"No."

"Looks like you."

"That's the idea."

"His hair's darker."

"I plan on dyeing mine."

"This guy ain't dead, is he? This ain't gonna come back and bite my ass?"

"He's very much alive. Back home in Holland by now."

At least he was alive when I left him in the back of a cab two weeks before. He was my appetizer, the first taste of an evening. I was seeing him home after he'd taken sick at an Irish bar off Fifth. We'd shared a pitcher of microbrew I'd dosed.

"You know, a passport's easier to fake than a driver's license. Fucked up, huh? Cheaper too."

"Then let's go with that. I really only need it for staying in hotels," I said.

"You know the Greek diner at Lex and 51st?"

"I can find it."

"Meet me there around this time Thursday. Let me have five hundred now. I'll have what you need."

I peeled off enough fifties. He folded them inside the Dutch passport and squirreled that away inside the last Members Only jacket in the known world.

"Where you want me to drop you? I got a thing on Long Island," he said.

"14th is coming up. I'll get out there."

"Thursday. Round this time. Greek place on Lex," he said as a goodbye before turning around to head back onto the drive.

I made my way west toward clubland. The thirst had me in its grip.

• 39 •

The Bolivar was no one's idea of a luxury hotel. To me it was heaven after months of living like a bum, sleeping anywhere that I knew would remain sunless during the daytime hours.

The rooms were closets and the staff was made up of an extended family of Pakistanis. One surlier than the next. The sheets were changed daily if I wanted but I rarely wanted. There was a stout in-room safe for my loot. And the room was as dark as a tomb with a single window facing a narrow airshaft. The sun rarely reached farther than the sill from the opening five stories above. Shades and thick draperies in an ornate damask pattern shut even that out. For privacy a Do Not Disturb sign in eight languages hung from the doorknob as a permanent fixture. And the occasional twenty slipped to the desk clerk kept the maid from knocking on the door during daytime hours.

The owner/manager was Mr. Khan, and I arranged for a monthly rate charged to my brand new Amex card in the name of Allen Townsend. The same name was on my passport which had me as a native of Ottawa, Canada. The monthly Amex bills were sent to a box I held at a place that kept my hours called Going Postal on Houston. I could pay the bill in cash at an ATM.

Located off Union Square, the Bolivar was central to my hunting grounds with the subway handy if I felt like spreading out a little. Having a secure place to sleep took a lot of pressure off. That's not to say that I could relax. I was still an addict, the hunger is what drove me. There was no room for pleasure or distraction in this life I was leading. The best I could do was satisfaction, to quench the thirst. But when the sleep wore off and the night came down, I was on the hunt again.

I had it knocked. I was set. I was living as well as I could, given the restrictions and conditions forced on me. A place to coop. More than enough cash to cover my, by Manhattan standards, meager expenses. And more cash added to the pile by the high rollers I ran into at the clubs. Even if simple embarrassment didn't stop them from going to the cops, I wasn't in much danger. I was invisible to surveillance cameras. There was no recorded evidence to back up anyone's statement. I was a ghost. Smoke.

It all went smooth like that for two or three months.

Summer was coming on and I decided it was past time I traveled out to Brooklyn again. New clubs. New faces. Fresh blood. I slipped on a new silk suit over a cotton pullover and cabbed over to a hot new place with a Bollywood theme.

A new club brought the densest crowd. Lots of Anglos mixed with an Asian crowd and all dancing to a Sufi beat played by a DJ in a booth that sat in the lap of a three-story papier-mâché statue of Ganesh. You know the one. Hindu god who looks like a big gay elephant. I made a wedge of my hands to wriggle through the five-deep mob at the longer of two bars. I scanned the crowd, looking for anyone who might already be way past the legal limit.

I sensed a movement to my right. Some cross words from a dark man in a white suit aimed at someone I couldn't see yet. He stepped aside with a muttered curse to allow a slender woman to take her place at the bar close by me. I didn't pay attention at first.

A hand laid atop mine where it rested on the curve of leather upholstery that ran along the bar top. I knew those fingers, ghostly white in the garish light of the strobes set in the ceiling. I turned to her to ask if she wanted a drink. She looked much the same. Of course she did. Her hair was longer now with blunt cut bangs and a streak of white dyed above a brow. Her smile was more of a knowing smirk than an expression of pleasure, judging me with those coal black eyes.

Roxanne would never change.

· 40 ·

We took a booth away from the noise. She tinkled the ice in the drink I bought her and eyed me with a tilted smile.

"I hardly recognize you," she said.

"The hair? I needed to match the guy in my photo ID," I said.

"*Non, mon petit*. It's more than that. You have adapted. You are one of us now."

"Not like I had a choice. You ran off and left me."

"I did not get far."

"They caught you? The guys who killed that cop? Why do you still have *your* head?"

"I paid a price." She pulled her hair aside to show me where her left ear had been cut. Rough white skin surrounded her ear canal.

"They let you live?"

"On their terms. So long as I behave I can be a part of the Order. I was away too long. The life of a rogue is tiring."

"This sounds like you're here to recruit me. The Order? Is this that Vikram guy?"

She reached out and took my hand.

"You have drawn attention to yourself. You have stayed too long in one place."

"I've been playing it careful. No one's looking for me."

"You are wrong, *mon petit*. Those four men you killed. The police are very interested."

"I haven't seen it mentioned in the news."

"They do not know what we know. You left fingerprints. The fingerprints of a man who was pronounced dead almost a year ago. A man whose body was stolen. You killed that morgue attendant. They are beginning to connect these events."

"I'll move on then," I said. It was a lie. I had no intention of leaving my current set-up.

"It may be too late for that," she said. Her eyes shifted to look past me.

I turned to see two men, big men, separate themselves from the crowd at the edge of the dance floor. Leather jackets, mean faces and something European, darkly Mediterranean, about them. They came straight for us. I started to rise. Roxanne's grip on my hand tightened. Her long nails dug deep into the flesh. I tried to yank away to slide from the booth. She pulled harder to trap me against the table. Then the two big men had their hands on me.

They worked together to haul me free and carry me through the packed horde of party animals. We were out in the street with each taking an arm to carry me, feet dangling, into the summer night. Roxanne followed. A valet pulled a Lincoln up to meet us at the curb. One of the big guys pitched me in the back seat and joined me, a huge hand with a firm grip on the back of my neck. The other big guy slid behind the wheel. Roxanne rode shotgun. We pulled from the curb with a jerk and were into traffic inside a second.

The guy with a vise grip on me held me pushed down onto the seat. My face was pressed into the leather. I could hear traffic and road noise but couldn't see where we were going.

"I am curious, *mon petit*," Roxanne said.

"Do we need to talk?" I said. I had to speak from the corner of my mouth, my nose mashed to the seat.

"It is a bit of a long drive."

"Fuck you." The hand pressed harder, sealing my mouth closed.

"You only feed from men. Is that intentional? Instinctual? Were you a homosexual in life? I never got that impression."

I muttered into the leather. I'd fed off a few girls. Never kept score. Never thought about it.

"It was not a conscious decision, was it? Perhaps there is enough of the male in you to see feeding as a conquest. A matter of domination."

The metallic flick of a lighter. The car filled with the smell of a cigarette. I heard her inhale sharply.

"Or is it that you are still the gentleman? Deferring to *la femme*? Still seeing women as the weaker gender? Something to be protected rather than preyed on?"

I could hear the shoosh-shoosh sound of tires on metal grating. We were on a bridge now. Jersey or Connecticut. Not back to Manhattan.

"A part of you refuses to surrender to your new nature, to fully become what you are. You resist becoming a monster. Feeding on the weak and helpless. That's how you see us, *non*? Monsters."

Truck traffic. Big wheels thundering by, blocking out the light through the car windows.

"It is all nature. We are part of nature. Like bacteria or mold. The lion does not hunt the strongest of a herd of zebra. The lion goes after the weak, the slow, the old. In the same way that we prey on the unwanted, the forgotten. Humanity has its discarded people. They are our prey."

The big car canted as it went into a long curving section of road. An exit ramp. We were over the river and coming off the bridge.

"But you have decided that you are some sort of gourmet. You decided that you will feed on more privileged fare. You left behind victims who had a place in society. That was bound to be noticed. Some of your prey overcame their embarrassment of being drugged and bled. They found police who would believe their mad stories. Especially as more and more were telling the same story."

The lights coming through the windows were less and less frequent until there were no lights at all. The car was rolling through darkness. No sound from outside except the wind rushing by.

"I liked you. You were clever. Too clever, as it turns out. *Je suis désolé, mon petit.*"

She was sorry.

• 41 •

The road surface under us got rougher and the ride along with it. I could hear something brushing the sides of the car. We were deep in tall grass. The car slewed to a stop. The doors at the front opened. The car rocked as Roxanne and the driver stepped outside. My minder took a new grip on my left arm and lifted me upright. The door by him swung open. My hand dug in my pocket for the revolver.

I pulled it and stuck it in the face of the guy who held me. I squeezed the trigger twice, shooting out both of his eyes. Two bloodless holes in his face looked like gouges in wet dough. He released my neck, howling in rage. I kicked out at him with both feet to send him sprawling to the ground. The revolver in my fist, I fired three more shots through the open door. There was a grunt then another as bullets found meat. I had a handle on the door and rolled out on the other side to thrash upright in grass as high as my chest.

Then I ran.

With the car at my back I ran full out through the grass. I was somewhere out in the wilds of New Jersey. It could have been the savannas of Africa if not for the shadow of the Pulaski Skyway blotting out the stars a mile off. There were lights on some kind of smoke stack on the horizon. And a conga line of passenger jets thrummed overhead on their way to a landing on a runway at Newark.

I could hear voices. Roxanne's above the others. Doors slammed and the Lincoln roared to life.

My shoes slapped through mud and then ankle deep water.

I pitched the empty revolver away and headed deeper into the marshy ground, ducked low in the grass.

The lights of the Lincoln washed over me ahead of the engine roar. I ran on, bent low, jinking to my right out of the harsh glare of the high beams. The water was up to my calves now.

I heard a clunk behind me followed by the whine of spinning wheels. The Lincoln was stuck. The beam from its lights shimmied back and forth across the top of the grass stalks as the big car fought to free itself.

I kept on, not looking back. I could hear Roxanne's voice rise to a shriek as she called after me. She stood on top of the stalled car shouting phrases I never learned in high school French. She was a lioness roaring out her rage and frustration at the prey that got away.

The miles of marshlands led to a river. I crossed it by walking the river bed to the other side. A chain link fence surrounded a yard of oil storage tanks. There were ribbons of pink streaking the sky. No time to feed. I needed to find a place out of the light.

I spent the day asleep in a cargo container abandoned alongside a rail siding. I woke up hungry. I hadn't fed the night before. I was miles from anywhere and followed the rail tracks toward the glimmer of the city reflected from the dark clouds above. It began to rain as if to enhance my mood. It would explain my wet clothes anyway.

There was no going back to the Bolivar. Chances were they knew about that. First place they'd look. I would need to go to ground, give myself time to come up with a brand new plan. New York was done for me. I'd need to find new hunting grounds or stay on the move a while. Maybe work my way west to Chicago or even California.

But first I needed to feed. The fire in my belly was a swirling ball of need. Heaven help the first soul I came across. Man or woman. Roxanne was right about that.

I *was* a monster.

I needed to start owning that.

· 42 ·

A girl in a McDonald's polo shirt was taking a cigarette break at a picnic table set up at the rear of a parking lot. She was talking in Spanish on a bejeweled cell.

She didn't see or hear me coming out of the hedges behind her. I planted a hand on the back of her head and drove her face into the table top. I lifted her from the bench and raised her body over my head to throw her over a concrete block wall that surrounded a pair of dumpsters. I vaulted in after her.

She lay by a dumpster, stunned with a bloody crease in her forehead. A pathetic mewling came from between broken teeth. I used the carpet knife to cut away a leg of her uniform slacks. Another slash opened the femoral artery on the inside of her thigh. I drank until she was dead white. Lips and fingertips blue. I tipped her into a dumpster labeled for cardboard only and shifted a few flattened boxes to cover her.

I jumped back over the wall and picked up the cell phone left on the picnic table and tossed it far over the hedges. I walked through the double line of cars at the drive-thru and into the McDonald's at the entrance nearest the rest rooms.

Seated in a stall I did an inventory of what was left in my pockets. A pool of muddy water spread on the tile where it dripped from my soaked clothes. I still had a wad of cash, my phony passport and wallet.

I needed to get back to the city. I needed dry clothes and a place to hide. There was no going back to the Bolivar. They'd know about that. I had to assume that. Thousands in cash and my stash of soporifics were lost to me. I'd have to find another place. But first I needed a few nights in the city to set everything up.

It was going to be a long night. But the hunger was satisfied for now.

A cab took me to Newark Station and I caught a train into the city. I found a mostly empty car. I stank of the river mud soaked into my clothes.

At the K-Mart in Penn Station I bought some dry clothes, sneakers and a new carpet knife with a pack of fresh blades. The old knife was wet. It would begin to rust.

I changed in a men's room stall, shoving the wet clothes into a K-Mart bag and the bag into a trash bin.

The hunger was satisfied for now and it was still early evening. I walked down to 42nd to a multiplex. I bought a ticket for some cartoon movie and moved from theater to theater only staying a few minutes in each. Kind of a forlorn hope but I was hoping to find Lissa in the audience. I settled down in the last theater to watch some mindless movie with lots of car crashes. When it was over I left the theater to cruise the street down to a bookstore Lissa liked to browse. She wasn't there.

The night moved toward morning. The traffic was all trucks coming into the city on deliveries. I walked back to Penn Station and hopped off the end of a platform into the tunnels.

The L.I.R.R. trains still sat derelict on that siding. I shooed rats aside to lie down on a bench with the least damage. I rested my head back on the stack of newspapers lying there and looked up at the folded blanket spread on the overheard luggage rack. I wondered where she was cooping tonight. There was still time before dawn and I hoped she'd come back.

In the dismal light I read a *Wall Street Journal* that was five years old. I dropped off halfway through an article about shifting trends in retail. My last thoughts were a confused mélange featuring Lissa and Roxanne. I didn't dream any more. But those thoughts, as I succumbed to the darkness, disturbed me. The blackness, when it washed over me, came with an unpleasant thrill of unease.

· 43 ·

I found her the next night.

Or what remained of her.

I breakfasted on a junkie I found nodding at the bottom of the steps down to the platform on 51st. Then I wandered the tunnels north. Somewhere after the Hunter College stop I saw something flash white along the tracks in the lights from a local rattling to a stop at 77th.

It was the white cotton dress we bought for her. It lay in the filth against a wall of the tunnel. It was collapsed onto scorched remnants of her bones. Tiny wrists and ankles, burnt crusty black, were still wrapped in loops of chains locked tight around two support girders. Directly above were the lights and the sounds of the sidewalks on Lexington coming down through a long steel grate.

She was the lamb now.

Someone chained her here and left her for the sunshine to come down from above. The early morning light would be muted as it rose behind the buildings. The full burning glare of it would take hours to reach the grates above.

She would have spent hours sick and afraid, waiting to be turned to ash by the killing light. She couldn't call out. She couldn't free herself. And the ones who left her here would be gone to their own roosts to sleep through what they left her to endure.

I stooped to pick up the dress and shake the cold embers from it. I bunched it in my fist and shoved it under my shirt.

Roxanne never asked how I knew about Vikram. She wasn't surprised when I said his name. She didn't ask where I'd heard it. She already knew. Lissa was gone even before Roxanne found me. Lissa was *how* Roxanne found me. While I slept cozy in my room at the Bolivar, Lissa was slowly being exterminated in this shitty place.

I needed to run and run far. It was too late that night to think about relocating. I'd need a place to hide in the city. It had to be a place I'd never cooped before.

I started north again. An express was thundering up the tunnel behind me and I stepped onto the ballast between tracks to let it pass. The lights from the lead car struck a row of supports. They cast a shadow on the face of a girder. The shadow of a man that ducked out of sight too late. Everything about the shadow's movement was wrong. It wasn't a wastoid or a junkie. It moved with purpose to hide.

It moved like a predator.

A side tunnel leading down to the Metro North tracks was behind me. I ran to it. I could hear a pair of feet crunching gravel behind me. I raced along the westbound passage tunnel, sliding down concrete steps that led deeper toward the commuter tunnels that travelled out to the bedroom counties and Connecticut. The feet scuffed behind me. Only one pursuer for now. The one they left behind to stake out Lissa's remains, hoping I'd find her eventually.

After months of wandering underground I had the advantage of my knowledge of the world that lies beneath the city. I could lose him before any more showed up to help him. I came out on a narrow ledge that ran along the pair of tracks the Metro North trains ran on. The tracks went north where they came out of the earth above 97th Street. I vaulted the guardrail to drop down onto the lane by the tracks. I raced south, deeper into the system heading back toward Grand Central and the endless warren of tunnels that branched out from there like the strands of a spider web.

Footfalls behind me sprayed gravel. I turned to see the shadow figure move under the cone of radiance from a lamp above. It was one of the Eurotrash thugs that were with Roxanne. The driver. He came after me in a machine-like jog.

It was going to be a long stretch until I reached Grand Central. No side tunnels for another hundred yards. A big bastard, his stride was longer than mine. He'd catch up to me before then. Simple math. I was moving as fast as I could. His feet spattered stones behind me. I leapt the nearest rail to run along the smoother surface of concrete ties. That put a hitch in his step as he adjusted to the uneven surface. But he fell into a rhythm after a half dozen steps and was gaining on me again.

The rails far ahead of me winked with silver flashes. A ball of light rose from the artificial horizon in a mock sunrise. The ties under me trembled and the rails hummed. A train was coming down the track we were on.

I began making long leaps, taking three ties at a time toward the glowing ball of light. The thug fought to keep up. He stumbled once and caught himself. He raced to close the gap.

The glare in front of me expanded to fill my vision. The roar of its approach filled my ears. A horn blared above the thunder, a long blast warning us to clear the tracks. I kept moving, leaping, toward the light growing higher and higher as the train raced up the slight grade of the tracks.

The thug was close. The fingertips of his outstretched hand brushed my shoulder. I flinched from his grip. He barked a huff of frustration. A new burst of speed gave him a solid grip on the sleeve of my jacket. I twisted, freeing my arm from the sleeve. I continued the twist, pulling him from his feet. The jacket came off my shoulders. I tripped, rolled and was off the tracks as the train blasted by. I came to rest on the gravel near the other track line.

Not so lucky the big thug. The engine hit him straight on doing fifty. What part of him wasn't dismembered on first impact was chewed to bits under the steel wheels of the next six cars. The train would take another mile or so to come to a stop. The engineer would be on the radio to his bosses and that would bring the transit cops.

I trotted along between the tracks to reach Grand Central and the freedom of the tunnels. The thug was scattered everywhere. A leg here. An arm there. Ropey lengths of shiny black guts stretched between bits of chopped torso. Finally there was the head regarding me with a white hot rage. The lips worked to make words but all that came out was a wet hissing sound. As I ran by I kicked out and sent the head tumbling away over the tracks into the shadows between two lamps.

The end of a platform sat under blinking fluorescents. I climbed the steel steps and made my way into the station. I crossed the enormous vaulted cathedral of Grand Central's main station and joined an after-theater crowd for the descent to the subway platforms.

I sat on a bench and waited for the next train to arrive and the platform to empty. People rushed on and off the cars until the platform was clear. The train pulled away and all was silent.

But I wasn't alone. A woman rose from a bench farther along the station to walk toward me. Hands in the pockets of her coat, a tilted smile on her lips.

I hadn't been running away from anyone.

I'd been running toward Roxanne.

· 44 ·

The long blade of a machete dropped from the sleeve of her coat. She had a professional grip on the handle, her glove leather creaked as her fingers tightened around it. She held it down by her leg so that it wasn't visible to the people on the opposite platform.

I backed away, eyes locked on her. The eyes were dead glass. The tilted smile frozen. I turned and ran to the end of the platform, leaping a chain barrier down to the track level. I trotted into the dark on legs that could never weary. She followed like a shadow, matching me step for step. She spoke as she followed, her voice reaching from the dark behind me.

"You blinded Anton. Did you know? I told you that we do not heal. We only endure. I ended him as I will end you. Ours is no world for the weak, *mon petit*."

"What's the other asshole's name?" I shouted down the tunnel.

"Paolo. Did you lose him in the tunnels?"

"Last time I saw him the Waterbury Express had turned him to hamburger." I barked out a laugh.

"*Cochon!*" She shrieked it.

"Get you in trouble with the boss, bitch?"

I left her there to leap through uprights that ran between the tracks. A train was sweeping toward us. I jumped the tracks just ahead of it to put the train between us. The rushing cars only an arm's length away, I raced back the way I'd come to a steel ladder bolted to the wall. I was halfway up the rungs by the time the train passed under me.

I could hear Roxanne's cry of frustration as I crawled out of a ventilation hatch to the floor above. I was in some kind of service corridor. Concrete floor and tiled walls. Atop the hatch opening was a six foot long steel grate hinged open and secured in place on a hook. I straddled the opening and looked down to see Roxanne standing below, her hands and one booted foot on the rungs.

"You are a child. You act as a child does. I might have taught you our ways but we will never know now." She shrugged. Indifferent. Those black eyes immobile on mine.

"I *was* a child. Born again in a seriously fucked up way thanks to you."

Her eyes narrowed to slits.

"Why did you have to do that to Lissa? To get back at me? Or didn't she fit Vikram's idea of what a blood-sucking freak should be?"

"She did not suit the order of things. She was small and weak just as you are stupid and weak. For the Order to continue requires darkness. *Hor la loi* like you risk bringing us all into the light. And there are more kinds of light than the sun, *mon petit*."

"We're monsters. Worse than that. We're a disease."

"And what is a germ? *Une bactérie*? We are a form of life. Like a flower or a moth. We are part of nature and have been for thousands of years."

"You're dead, Roxanne. You really need to start acting like it."

She came up the ladder with a roar from deep inside. Teeth bared and eyes wide with rage. When she was at the top rungs I unhooked the steel grate from the wall and pulled it free. A quarter ton of steel grate dropped into place with a meaty thud. I jumped on it to add my weight to the mass.

Roxanne was caught, pinned, with one arm and her head above the vent opening. The hard edge of the grate bit halfway through her neck like the blade of a blunt guillotine. Her arm was severed clean off inside the coat sleeve. The machete clattered to the floor, her hand still firm on the handle. Her eyes rolled to look up at me standing atop the grate that was crushing what was left of her throat.

Her lips formed words through the bubbling black bile that filled her mouth.

I leaned down close, trying to catch the last words she would ever speak.

"*J'ai vu mourir les éléphants.*"

I looked it up later. It meant "I watched the elephants die."

Or maybe I heard it wrong.

· 45 ·

Seattle only has sunshine one out of three days. Doesn't help me much. But it was a place to go that was far from New York. And they're tolerant of all kinds of homeless, transients and freaks out here.

I've been here a month, living off the cash I left in the room safe at the Bolivar. Changed my mind about going back there after Roxanne and her friends were gone.

Spent part of the money on a new identity. I'm Alan Chandler from Evansville, Indiana now. Shaved my head to match the photo I had. Can't undo that. That's the mood I'm in. Nothing lasts forever. Even me.

I have a laptop, a smart phone, a modem and a van. I stay mobile, moving from one WiFi hot spot to another.

Signed up for Twitter, Facebook, Google, Instagram, Tumblr, Kick, Slap, and Poke. Used my real name. The name I was born with. The name I used when I was alive. I filled out all the applications the same way. Under occupation I typed:

Vampire

I put links on all my accounts to a blog page where I told my story. I included a selfie video I made. I'm not in the video and that's the point. It shows me feeding off some wasted college student from Cornish. More accurately, some invisible something draining the life from a catatonic girl lying naked in an alley. I took her clothes off to make sure it went viral.

When I lay down to coop in my van that first morning I had ten hits on Facebook and five on Twitter. When I woke up the next night I had eight thousand followers on Facebook, close to ten thousand on Twitter. Same story on other sites along with hundreds of shares. Within three days the conspiracy sites linked to my blog and added blogs of their own connecting back to the case of the missing corpse. By the end of the week the *Enquirer* picked it up on their site and by the following week in print. Page one. They did the homework to uncover my connection to a string of murders in New York.

DEAD MAN'S PRINTS AT HOMICIDE SCENE

One by one my accounts were shut down. That's okay. This has taken on a life of its own. The cable news channels ran with it. They interview so-called experts and detectives and scientists. Some think it's fake. Some think there's some truth to it. Some buy it all the way. But they're all talking about it. I was trending. I was relevant.

Like Roxanne said, there's more kinds of light than the sun.

Only a matter of time now.

I wonder who'll find me first.

Chuck Dixon is the prolific author of thousands of comic book scripts for *Batman and Robin, the Punisher, Nightwing, Conan the Barbarian, Airboy, the Simpsons, Alien Legion* and countless other titles.

Together with Graham Nolan, Chuck created the now iconic Batman villain Bane. He also wrote the international bestselling graphic novel adaptation of J.R.R. Tolkien's *The Hobbit*.

He currently writes two series for Bruno Books: the time travel epic Bad Times, as well as the ebook sensation Levon Cade. His zombie apocalypse novel *Gomers* is set to start production as a feature film in the fall of 2016. He also adapted Peter Schweitzer's controversial bestseller *Clinton Cash* into a graphic novel.

He calls Florida home these days.

Visit the Dixonverse!
www.dixonverse.net

WHEN THE DEAD WALK THE EARTH...
...THE LIVING GO SHOPPING.

Jim and Smash are looking for a safe place to sit out the zombie armageddon. They choose a giant home improvement store as their sanctuary. But an Afghanistant war vet and an attack dog with gender issues have already claimed the place.

And then there's the girl...

Made in the USA
Columbia, SC
08 October 2017